LETTERS FROM ALCATRAZ

LETTERS FROM ALCATRAZ:

40 YEARS LATER

Tina Westbrook

Order this book online at www.trafford.com
or email orders@trafford.com

Most Trafford titles are also available at major online book retailers.

Printed in Victoria, BC, Canada.

ISBN: 978-1-4269-2614-3 (sc)
ISBN: 978-1-4269-2613-6 (dj)

Library of Congress Control Number: 2010901425

*We at Trafford believe that it is the responsibility of us all, as both individuals
and corporations, to make choices that are environmentally and socially sound.
You, in turn, are supporting this responsible conduct each time you purchase a
Trafford book, or make use of our publishing services. To find out how you are
helping, please visit www.trafford.com/responsiblepublishing.html*

*Our mission is to efficiently provide the world's finest, most comprehensive
book publishing service, enabling every author to experience success.
To find out how to publish your book, your way, and have it available
worldwide, visit us online at www.trafford.com*

Trafford rev. 02/10/2010

Trafford PUBLISHING® www.trafford.com

North America & international
toll-free: 1 888 232 4444 (USA & Canada)
phone: 250 383 6864 ♦ fax: 812 355 4082 ♦ email: info@trafford.com

For "Mr. Alcatraz"

Inside that tiny box were the words that I had wanted to say to Diana, but never quite got them out. A silver, heart shaped locket said it for me.

Engraved on the front of the locket was "I love you."

Chapter 1
Escape Proof

Good Morning Tina!

Welcome to what I hope is a long and mutual friendship. This site is not just for alumni classmates. This is a place where we can all come together, share stories, photo's, reconnect with old friends and build new relationships. It is good to open your heart and mind to new people, new friendships and new experiences. From the moment I stumbled across your photo's in the photography group I knew we would get along just fine. For we have something in common; Alcatraz!

May your guardian angel always walk with you!

Your friend,
C.J

As I boarded the plane I found myself wishing that I had booked a flight that originated in Birmingham and not one that was simply picking up more passengers. Those that were already on the plane appeared quite comfortable and as I made my way to my seat I noticed the look of irritation creeping up on some passengers faces. They acted as if their entire lives were being inconvenienced by the person that had purchased the seat next to them.

Row 10 seat B is where I would be spending the next six hours. As I approached row 10 I immediately took notice of the two gentlemen that I would be sandwiched between. The gentleman sitting in the aisle seat looked up and smiled.

"Excuse me...I'm sorry" was all I could think to say.

Mr. Aisle seat stood up and let me in. *Thank God I didn't bring any carry on luggage! Just my purse and my file folder!*

I sat down, fastened my seat belt and placed my purse under the seat in front of me. The flight attendant began her usual pre-flight instructions and I suddenly found myself becoming irritated. The gentleman sitting in the window seat next to me was reading his newspaper, but he wasn't reading it to himself, he was reading it out loud! Not so loud that the entire plane could hear him, but loud enough that *I* could hear him. I momentarily closed my eyes wishing that he would shut the hell up.

Once in the air, Mr. Aisle seat lowered his tray and placed his lap top on it. I quickly realized that I would need to occupy my time or continue to listen to Mr. Window seat read the entire *Marietta Daily Journal.*

1

As I ran my hands across the file folder that was resting in my lap I was reminded of two of my favorite quotes: *Life is not measured by the number of breaths we take, but by the number of moments that take our breath away.* I have no idea who first said those words, but they have stayed with me since hearing them. My other favorite quote came from C. J. He wrote these words in one of his e-mail messages and I have never forgotten them. *To leave this world having not expressed how you feel is sad, but to live in this world and not express how you feel is a tragedy.*

I opened the file folder and began to read.

04/28/06

Thank you Tina for sharing your story and photo albums! I too have taken many photos of Alcatraz during the period of 1966 to 1971. My Father in Law was a penal officer on Alcatraz. After the prison closed in 1963 he and his wife remained on the island until 1971. They were contracted by GSA as caretakers of the property. I will never forget the first night I spent on Alcatraz. It was a very foggy night and the fog horn kept blasting all night long; every 30 seconds. At that time I was dating Diana, Jake's youngest daughter. The year was 1966. Many weekends Diana and I would spend leisure time on Alcatraz visiting her mom and dad. It was easy to get lost in time while being in the center of the San Francisco Bay. It truly is paradise. In those days a 300 yard off limit regulation was posted, if offended action was required.

Here's a pic from Alcatraz 1971. This was the last time I was on the island.

I will write again soon.

Take care,
C.J.

Reading that first letter from C. J. about his time at Alcatraz filled me with excitement. I have been intrigued and fascinated with Alcatraz since seeing the movie "Escape From Alcatraz" in 1980. I was fifteen years old at the time and the movie left me wanting more. *What ever happened to the men that escaped? Did they get off the island and begin new lives, or did they drown as many suspected? If they did drown, why were their bodies never recovered?* I chose to believe that they truly escaped. They made it across the icy waters and disappeared; never to be heard from again.

It was March 1999 when I visited Alcatraz for the first time. Although I was excited to spend time in San Francisco, and experience this place that I had heard so much about, I was ecstatic about going to Alcatraz. I would walk the corridors of Alcatraz. I would see where and how the inmates of Alcatraz lived. I would, with my very own eyes, see how they escaped.

It was a very cold day and there was a light mist. I remember thinking *how cold is that water?* and then wondering how cold it was when the inmates escaped. Add to that the fact that it was night time and that was no short swim. *Could they make it?*

As I boarded the ferry I began to feel chilled to the bone. I vividly remember shaking and praying that we got to the island quickly. The wind was whipping through my hair and the water gently sprayed me. I removed my camera from my camera bag and attempted to get as many shots as possible. The entire time I was attempting to shoot I mumbled to myself. I was mad at myself for bringing such a large camera. I was mad because my hair kept flying into the lens. And, because I was shooting with film, I had no idea if any of the photographs would be worth the paper that they would be printed on. I finally calmed myself down by telling myself that I would get better shots once off the ferry. And, the real *treat* would be inside the prison. That's where everything happened.

As I exited the ferry I was filled with anticipation and excitement. My mind was racing and I couldn't hear anything that anyone was saying. It was as if my imagination took over and no one else was around. I immediately thought of the inmates that served time at Alcatraz. As they arrived on the island what were they thinking? For a moment, a very brief moment, I could visualize Al Capone stepping off a ferry and thinking *you have got to be kidding me*. What *would* someone think? Alcatraz had been billed as escape proof.

In 1962 three men disappeared from Alcatraz. Whether they lived to tell the tale remains a mystery. Frank Morris, Clarence Anglin, and his brother John escaped from Alcatraz on June 11, 1962. Their daring escape was made famous by the movie "Escape From Alcatraz", which starred Clint Eastwood and was directed by Don Siegel. Prison Authorities concluded that all three escapees had drowned, but their bodies were never recovered. Undoubtedly the most famous escape, but this was not the first escape from *The Rock*.

Alcatraz Island was seized by the United States in 1846. Work began on fortifications in 1853 and in 1857 a citadel was constructed. In 1861 the fort was designated as the official U.S. Army prison for the western states and territories. Between 1908 and 1911 the citadel was demolished and replaced by the present reinforced concrete cellhouse.

The most successful escape from Alcatraz occurred on November 28, 1918. Four prisoners managed to escape with rafts. The authorities assumed they had drowned in the San Francisco Bay, but they later appeared in Sutro Forest. One of the prisoners was recaptured, leaving the remaining three unaccounted for.

In 1934 Alcatraz was converted into a Federal prison. The old military prison was upgraded and equipped with the latest *"escape-proof"* safeguards. Authorities were convinced that the treacherous waters of the San Francisco Bay would be a major barrier to those who attempted to escape. However, in 1933, one year before converting the old military prison, three girls were able to prove that it wasn't impossible to swim across the bay successfully.

On December 16, 1937, just three years after Alcatraz was converted into a Federal prison Theodore Cole and Ralph Roe disappeared from Alcatraz. They were never seen again. Four years later a reporter from the San Francisco Chronicle declared they were still alive and living in South America.

Twenty five years to the day that Cole and Roe escaped John Paul Scott would make the last escape from Alcatraz. At the age of 35 John Paul Scott swam from the island to Fort Point, under the southern part of the Golden Gate Bridge, proving that it could be done by a convict.

Alcatraz Federal Penitentiary was officially closed on March 21, 1963.

As a Military Prison there have been eighty documented attempted escapes in twenty nine separate attempts. Sixty two of the men were caught, one may have drowned and seventeen are unknown.

As a Federal Penitentiary and from a total of 1,033 inmates, thirty four men had attempted to escape in fourteen separate attempts. Twenty three were caught, six were shot and killed, and five are missing. Prison authorities assumed the five missing men drowned.

On October 12, 1972 Alcatraz became part of the Golden Gate National Recreation Area and is currently managed by the National Park Service.

Chapter 2
Falling in love with
Diana and Alcatraz

05/04/06

Hello Tina,

Here's hoping you're well. I've been giving much thought to my days spent at Alcatraz and it occurred to me that to tell the story properly you should know how I came to experience Alcatraz.

In 1966 I was 23 years old and dating a beautiful young lady, Diana. To this day I speak her name and feel the rush of excitement as I had as a young man.

I met Diana in San Francisco and it was surely a time that I, nor anyone that was alive in 1966 and living in the Bay area, will ever forget. Life was different than it is today. I truly feel privileged to have come into my own in a place as vibrant and alive as San Francisco. This is surely before your time, but there's a song "I left my heart in San Francisco" and it holds true for me.

Some do not believe in love at first sight, but as I locked eyes with Diana for the first time, I knew that love at first sight truly existed. For at that moment I fell in love and that love continues today. It has endured 40 years.

"Excuse me...Ma'am...excuse me" I looked over at Mr. Window seat. "I'm sorry to bother you, but I need to get up". Great...one hour of reading to everyone on the plane and he needs to get up. I swiveled my legs toward Mr. Aisle seat and let Mr. Window seat go past.

"Are you going to California for pleasure or business?" *Okay... now Mr. Aisle seat wants to strike up a conversation.*

"I'm not really sure how to answer that question. Pleasure I guess".

Mr. Aisle seat looked at me as if he didn't quite understand my reply. "I'm going to meet someone that I've been corresponding with for about a year or so".

Now looking even more puzzled he replied "Oh...internet relationship?"

In that moment I couldn't help myself but to laugh. *Internet relationship? Oh my God! He thinks I'm going to California to hook up with someone!* "No. Well, yes. I don't know how to answer that. I've been corresponding with someone, but it's not like *that!* The man that I'm going to meet is 63 years old. He's become a very dear friend". Mr. Aisle seat shook his head as if to say *Uh huh, I bet!* and then lowered his head and went back to reading his newspaper.

05/11/06

Hello Tina!

I'm keeping my promise as I said I would send you some personal accounts of my experience on Alcatraz Island. On Alcatraz one can barely hear the bustling city of San Francisco. During the day many boats would push the 300 yard off limit distance one could come within the island. Twice a year sailboats would race the San Francisco Regatta. It is a picture sight to see the bellowing sails as the boats tack close in a circular formation between the Golden Gate Bridge and Sausalito. On any given day one could see all different types of water craft pass by Alcatraz Island. The Navy has installations at Treasure Island and Alamedia. Ships such as battleships to flat top carriers and submarines would pass by.

In 1967 Diana and I were married on Alcatraz. All guests had to be approved by General Service Administrations. Guests were limited to one hundred and fifty. We invited mostly close friends and family. Because of the notoriety at the time many vendors agreed to perform services for free; just to have the privilege to come on the island. It was a big deal back then.

Flowers, entertainment, catering and transportation were provided close to nothing. Even the services from a local television station were provided at no cost. It was on their helicopter that Diana and I were lifted off the island as we waived goodbye from the air on that August 29, 1967 wedding day.

After returning from our honeymoon we discovered that the band had continued to play even after we left the island. To this day people continue to remark that it was the best wedding they have ever attended.

I will always regard that day as the best day of my life. One look at Diana is all I've ever needed to remind me that I was destined to love her.

I have lived a life that many people have only dreamed of. I have loved and been loved. Diana and I have grown together and sustained a loving relationship. The world has changed. Our country has changed. San Francisco has changed. Yet throughout the years, Diana has never changed. For that I am eternally grateful.

May God Bless you

C.J.

"I'm back...sorry...excuse me." Mr. Window seat has returned. As he sat back down I closed my file folder and decided to close my eyes; perhaps take a cat nap, but Mr. Window seat had other plans.

"Do you live in Birmingham?" he asked. I opened my eyes and explained to him that I live about an hour northwest of Birmingham.

"Oh, so what takes ya to California?"

Oh God! Not this again! "Well, I'm going to see a friend."

At that point Mr. Aisle seat chimed in "Not really a friend, is he? I mean, you don't even know this guy, right?"

Mr. Window seat looked at me as if I had horns growing out of my head and before I could open my mouth he said "You're going to see some guy you don't know?!" *Gee, thanks Mr. Aisle seat!*

"Not exactly. I mean, no, I don't know him. I've never met him, but we've been writing to each other for over a year now".

Mr. Window seat had an expression of concern on his face. "I don't get it. Why? This guy could be a serial killer for all you know, and you're meeting him by yourself? I hope you're meeting him in a public place. You know, people come up missing all the time after meeting up with someone they met on the internet."

Yep...Thanks Mr. Aisle seat! "It's not what you think. This gentleman is 63 years old. He's a friend that I've made a promise to and I intend on fulfilling that promise. Even if he is a serial killer!" Both just shook their heads and resumed their reading.

05/18/06

Good Morning My Dear Friend!

Here's hoping that today finds you well As I close my eyes and think back to 1966, the year that my life was forever changed, I realize that I have not shared with you "how" I met Diana. The date was August 29, 1966. This date is quite historical; that you will understand shortly.

The Beatles were performing at Candlestick Park, which is located in San Francisco. A very good friend of mine, sadly who has passed recently, had tickets and invited me to go with him. It was a Monday...I'm certain of that. There are some things that one never forgets, in spite of what seems to be an insignificant detail. Paul, John, George and Ringo had just taken the stage and I suddenly felt liquid running down my back. I turned to find the most beautiful woman I had ever laid eyes on looking at me as though she wished she were anywhere else in the world. She immediately apologized and explained that her hand had been bumped. I told her that it was okay and we laughed it off. During the 33 minutes that the Beatles performed I found myself looking back at this beautiful lady on several occasions.

The moment the concert was over I once again turned to the woman that spilled the drink on me and she asked if I had dried out. I replied that I had indeed and asked her if she enjoyed the show. We began talking about our love of music, and more importantly, our love of the Beatles. After a few minutes I asked her name. Diana. Her name was Diana. Without thinking about the possibility that this beautiful woman could reject me in front of one of my best friends, I asked her if I could call her sometime. She smiled, said yes, and casually removed an ink pen from her purse. She reached for my hand and wrote her phone number on my palm. With that she walked away with her friends and I endured an hour of harassment from my friend.

August 29, 1966 is the day that changed my life. I met the woman that I would love for eternity and I was a part of history. There was no way of knowing at that point in time, but this would be the Beatles very last concert. They played for 33 minutes and during those 33 minutes I fell in love with my future and said goodbye to my past.

Have a wonderful day my friend

C.J.

"Are you okay?" I looked over at Mr. Aisle seat and realized he was speaking to me.

"Yes, I'm okay, why do you ask?"

"I don't know. You look kind of sad. Like something that you're reading is bothering you".

What is this guy's problem? "No, I'm not sad. I think touched would be a better word" I replied.

"Does this have something to do with your pen pal?" *Is that sarcasm I hear in his voice?*

"I'm reading over some of his e-mails and he has a way of writing; a way of telling a story. Almost makes you feel like you were there".

Mr. Aisle seat looked me directly in the eye and a slight smile appeared. For a moment I was sure I would hear more sarcasm, but he lowered his eyes and with a shake of the head he said "A lot of people are good storytellers. My father's like that. He tells stories all the time. The problem with dad is you never know which one's are true and which one's are bullshit. He definitely has a way of telling stories!"

I sat there thinking about that for a brief moment and I smiled back at Mr. Aisle seat. I guess I could have left it at that, but sometimes my mouth overloads my brain. "Oh, so if your father was writing to someone, telling them stories, would you think he was going to do them any harm?"

Mr. Aisle seat smiled and replied "Point taken."

05/23/06

Hello Dear Tina!

I was watching the news last night and as usual, the headline was the Iraq War. I saw some footage of people protesting. Not sure where or when, but it reminded me of the protests that took place in 1967 regarding the Vietnam War. It's remarkable that as human's we never seem to learn from our past.

I was never what I, or anyone else for that matter, would consider "political". Diana, now that was a different story. She has a true love for anything political; always has. She was part of the movement. I was more of a spectator.

Diana attended the first "Human Be-In" that was held in Golden Gate Park during January of 1967. I'm sure of that date for two reasons; one being it occurred shortly after our first Christmas together, the second being a horrible event took place during that time. That's yet another story I will share with you at some point.

I do, however, remember April 15, 1967. That was the day 100,000 people marched from Second and Market Streets to Kezar Stadium at Golden Gate Park. Diana convinced me to go with her.

I closed my file folder filled with letters from C. J. and checked my watch. Realizing there were still four more hours to be spent in the air I decided to close my eyes and try to catch up on some much needed rest. Unfortunately, being on an airplane doesn't change anything. I haven't been able to sleep for more than a few hours at a time since last Wednesday and as I closed my eyes my mind continued to race.

What will it be like when C.J. and I come face to face for the first time? Will we shake hands? Will we greet each other with an awkward embrace? Or, will we throw our arms out and hug as one would do when finding a long lost friend?

As these thoughts raced through my mind it suddenly occurred to me: *What am I going to say? What is he going to say? What have I gotten myself into? Maybe going to San Francisco is a huge mistake! After all, I don't really know C. J. Could I have read him wrong? How do I know he's been telling me the truth? I don't know! What did Mr. Aisle seat say? Something about meeting in a public place? Or was that Mr. Window seat? Either or, good advice! I'm gonna take that advice! Oh God...I pray I'm doing the right thing!*

I managed to get an hour of sleep in before the flight attendant woke me up to ask me if I needed anything to drink. I wasn't aware that sleeping people needed anything to drink, but what the hell? "Yes. I'll take a vodka and orange juice."

Mr. Aisle seat perked right up "Vodka and orange juice? It's only 9:30. Getting an early start aren't you?" *I can't believe how quickly I had forgotten how funny this guy is.*

"Does it matter what time it is?" I spurted back.

"No. I don't guess it does. At least you're having orange juice with that vodka."

"Excuse me? How is this any of your business anyway?"

Mr. Aisle seat seemed a bit taken back. No, actually he seemed a bit hurt. I think I saw a twinge of hurt. "It isn't any of my business. Sorry I said anything."

OUCH! "Okay, look, I'm sorry. I didn't mean to snap at you. I'm just really tired and I guess I'm a bit on edge. I apologize."

Mr. Aisle seat grinned and replied "Apology accepted. I think you're going to like me before this flight is over."

With that having been said Mr. Window seat let out a chuckle and simply said "I doubt it."

They say everything happens for a reason. If that's true then I can't wait to find out the reason I was assigned to sit between these two.

06/01/06

Tina, Hello! I hope today is beautiful where you are. It's sunny in San Fran, which puts a spring in even an old mans step!

In October 1966 I made my first visit to Alcatraz. I was nervous, not because I was going to Alcatraz, but because I was to meet Diana's parents for the first time.

Diana and I had been dating for a little over a month and she was planning on visiting her parents for the weekend and invited me to tag along.

As the ferry approached the island Diana squeezed my hand and gently kissed me on my cheek. She was beaming and although it was rather chilly she seemed to radiate warmth. Her parents were standing at the dock and once off the ferry Diana extended her arms and the three embraced. A few moments passed and then Diana introduced me to her parents; Jake and Sandra. They were very welcoming and Jake made a comment that not many young men get to meet their girlfriends parents at Alcatraz. I remember thinking to myself, well, if they do, that may be a sign!

Now Tina, keep in mind that at this point in time Diana and I were still getting to know each other. We had been dating for a little more than a month and had only been out together six times. Every date had been better than the last, but we certainly had not been intimate. I say that because although I feel that a kiss is the most intimate moment between two people I understand that in the year 2006 a kiss is merely a kiss.

We had arrived on the island Friday afternoon and enjoyed a wonderful meal that Diana's mother had prepared for us. After a bit of chit chat and answering the questions that I assume most parents fire off to the young man that's dating their daughter, Diana and I went outside to explore the island

19

a bit and to enjoy the view. I had previously enjoyed the view from San Francisco to Alcatraz, but never had the opportunity to see San Francisco from Alcatraz. It truly was an amazing view.

Diana offered to show me around the inside of the prison, but I suggested we take the tour the next day; during daylight hours. She teased me a bit about not wanting to go into Alcatraz after dark, but it was all in good fun.

We were walking along the waters edge, hand in hand, when Diana turned to face me. She smiled and placed her hand on the side of my neck. As I lowered my head to kiss her she ran her hand through my hair.

My hands were now wrapped around her waist and our lips met. This was indeed the most sensual kiss I had ever experienced or even imagined experiencing. It was very soft and our lips barely touched. Diana began to softly kiss my neck and as I opened my eyes I realized that Alcatraz was looming above us.

Tina, it was in that very moment that I knew I was home. I was home with Diana and I was home at Alcatraz.

That night, after Jake and Sandra had turned in, Diana and I spent hours talking. It was very foggy that night and the fog horns blasted nonstop, every 30 seconds. It was that night that Diana and I made love for the first time. Although every time we have made love has been special, nothing has, nor ever could, compare to that first encounter. Many people assume that moments such as this have no real affect on men, or that we in some way minimize the importance of these moments in our lives. My dear friend, I can tell you with zero uncertainty that we are affected and we feel love as deeply as women do. We remember those moments in time and forever cherish them.

Thank you my dear friend for listening.

Thank you for taking this journey back in time with me.

C. J.

I closed the file folder and looked over at Mr. Window seat. Mr. Aisle seat chuckled. "What's so funny?" I asked.

"He's been snoring for thirty minutes. Are you just noticing?" I laughed and explained that I hadn't noticed.

"This guys letters must be fascinating. I've never seen anyone so absorbed in something the way you are with those letters."

I pondered that statement momentarily, and decided I would pick Mr. Aisle seats brain. "Have you ever met someone on the internet and felt a connection with them?"

Mr. Aisle seat smiled and said "Oh Yeah! I've met several people on the internet and felt a connection with them!"

What a waste of time! I should have known this guys mind would go straight to the gutter. I must have looked at him with a look of disgust because before I could get a word out he jumped right back in. "Look, I'm sorry. You're being serious and I'm making jokes. That's just what I do. Have I ever met someone on the internet and felt a connection? No. The answer is no. I've chatted with people through the internet and even flirted with several. But, I have never began or maintained any type of long term relationship with anyone that I met over the internet. By the way, what's your name?"

Hmmmm... "My name's Tina. What's yours?"

"Hi Tina, it's nice to meet you. I'm Chuck." We both smiled and then Chuck asked me what he really wanted to know.

"Okay, so you've never met this guy in person, and he's what? In his sixties? What can the two of you possibly be talking about that is so interesting that you would fly halfway across the country to meet up with him for? I seriously want to know because I'm not a bad looking guy, and I don't think there's anything that I could say to a woman that would get her so intrigued that she would take off to meet me." I couldn't help but to laugh. He was right about one thing...he's not a bad looking guy!

"Well, It's really hard to explain. Have you ever heard of Classmates? The web site?"

Chuck seemed to think about it for a second and kind of shook his head "Yeah, I think so. I've seen some advertising when I check e-mail. It says something like, what year did you graduate? Or, what state did you graduate in? Is that the site?"

"Yes, that's it! Okay, so about a year and a half ago I noticed the advertising and realizing that my twenty fifth reunion wasn't that far off I thought I would check out the site. See what ever came of some of the people I knew back then. I didn't realize that through that site you could meet people from all over the world. I thought I would just log into my school, and only have access to that one school. But it's not that way at all. Once you're in the Classmates web site they have all sorts of groups that you can join. So, being a photographer I checked out the photography group. Through Classmates I not only reconnected with some old high school friends, but I met a lot of new friends. People that otherwise I never would have had the opportunity to meet. The gentleman that I'm going to see in California is one of them. I met him through the photography group."

Chuck seemed to be letting all of that sink in before he commented. "Oh. Okay. But I still don't get it. If this isn't a romantic thing, and you have this stack of letters, why are you going to see him? Is he ill or something?"

Hmmmm... This is harder to explain than I thought it would be. "No, he's not ill. He's just going through a difficult time right now, and he asked me to come visit. It doesn't matter whether or not I've ever met him face to face before. I have probably learned more about him and his life than I have ever learned about some of my closest friends. When you spend a year communicating with someone, you begin to understand that person. People can discuss things in an e-mail that they would never discuss with family or even close friends. There's no fear of disappointing someone. No fear of rejection. He really is a very dear friend."

Chuck appeared to be very interested in what I was saying, but I thought it may be time to change the subject. "Hey, enough about me and my e-mail buddy. What takes you to California?"

"Hmmm...well, I'm originally from California. I moved to Atlanta five years ago. My company transferred me. Anyway, I'm going home for a memorial service."

I *wish I hadn't asked.* I've never been very good at moments like this. You never know if someone wants to talk about it, or if they're secretly wishing you hadn't asked. The only thing I knew to say was "I'm sorry to hear that."

Chuck smiled slightly. "That's okay. Don't be sorry. My mom passed away a year ago; she died unexpectedly. There was a memorial service after she died, but my dad wants to have another one. He said he was so out of it at the first one that he doesn't feel like he really said goodbye. We're just trying to make him happy."

The flight attendant came by and Chuck got her attention. "Hi. Can we get two vodka's with orange juice?"

I snickered and said "Kinda early for that, isn't it? Good thing you're getting orange juice to go with that vodka!"

Chuck and I spent the next hour chit chatting about work, photography, and traveling. I found Chuck to be quite interesting. Like me, he has traveled extensively; mostly for work, but he came across as having an adventurous spirit. I liked that.

06/07/06

Hello Friend! I hope today finds you well!

The story of Alcatraz and Diana continues...

Diana and I had our first date on September 2, 1966. It was five days after we met at Candlestick Park. I wanted to call her the same day I met her, but decided that may look a tad bit desperate, so I waited until the next day. Looking back now I think that too may have made me look desperate, but in my mind I was afraid that if I waited too long she may forget me.

That first telephone conversation was not at all how I expected it to be. There was no awkward silence, no thoughts of "what am I going to say?" We just talked. We talked about the concert, about our lives, about our families. We decided that we would go out on Friday night, September 2nd.

I was so excited to see this beautiful young lady again. I thought about bringing flowers, but not really knowing her I was worried that this may appear old fashioned. I offered to pick her up at her apartment, but she had another idea. We could meet again at Candlestick Park. That would be fun.7pm.

So, as planned, we met. Diana was simply stunning. She wore a blue skirt and a white blouse. Her long brown hair was pulled back and she wore a single strand of pearls. I have no recollection of what I was wearing. I'm quite positive that regardless of what I was wearing she out shined me.

I was so excited to be spending time with Diana. Our conversation flowed easily and before I knew it an hour had passed. We had walked at least 3 miles, just talking and getting to know each other. I asked Diana if she wanted to grab a bite and she agreed. We walked a bit longer and came across a small Italian Restaurant located on 2nd Street. It was very busy, but we managed to get a table after waiting a short 15 minutes. We enjoyed a wonderful meal and the conversation continued to flow easily.

We left the restaurant and headed back to Candlestick Park. Diana had told me that she lived very close to the area and I offered to walk her home. She agreed and we headed in that direction. As we approached her apartment building she smiled and thanked me for such a lovely evening. I told her that it was the most enjoyable evening I had experienced in some time and asked if I could call her again. She lowered her eyes and smiled. When she lifted her eyes she moved towards me and answered by placing a kiss on my cheek.

06/09/06

Dear Tina,

Thank you so much for your recent e-mail. I cannot remember the last time I laughed as much as I did reading that! You are truly a joy to know!

After my first trip to Alcatraz with Diana we began seeing each other much more frequently. Instead of once or twice a week it became as much as four or five times a week. Every weekend was spent together. Usually at my place because at her place there was very little privacy, as she shared her apartment with two of her girlfriends.

Our first weekend together was splendid. Diana arrived at my house on friday around 7PM. We went out that night; to a local club. There was a band playing and we danced the night away. After leaving the club we walked back home, laughing all the way.

Tina, I felt then, and I feel the same today; I was meant to spend my life with Diana. This may sound a bit cliche, but when I met her I just knew that I was put on this earth to love her.

My fondest memories are of those early years. We were young and unaware of what our future held, but we were ready to find out!

Diana and I made the most of our time together, and we continue to do so today. Our favorite day has always been Sunday. For on this day, we do nothing but enjoy each other. This "tradition" began that first weekend we were together after our visit to Alcatraz.

Sunday's have always been our day to sleep in, make breakfast together, and be lazy. Most Sundays after breakfast we would shower together and then pile up in bed. Read, listen to music, talk and spend endless hours making love.

I often wonder if couples today really enjoy each other as much as we always have. It seems that too many young people get caught up in outside influences and forget about what's really important.

Sometimes I can close my eyes and remember those early days as if it were yesterday. The smell of Diana's hair, the warmth of her body next to mine, her breath in my face; the innocence of a time long gone.

May you have a wonderful day,

C.J.

"Hey, Tina. What time is it?" I looked over at Chuck, checked my watch and told him that it was 11:40. We had been in the air for a little more than five hours. It wouldn't be much longer and I would be in San Francisco!

I promised C.J. that I would call him once I arrived at the hotel. My plans with C.J. aren't really plans. We talked about getting together the day after I arrived; C.J. was adamant about showing me around San Francisco, but we never made concrete plans. He knows I've been there before, but he seemed so excited to show me San Francisco through his eyes. It's obvious how much he loves that city. If the truth be known, I'm just as excited to see San Francisco through CJ.'s eyes as he is to show me. C.J. is so passionate about San Francisco that I often tease him about doing commercials for the Chamber of Commerce. I could see it now!

Hello! My name is C. J. and I want to invite you to San Francisco. The city by the bay! San Francisco has everything to offer! Won't you come along with me and discover what brings millions of visitors to our city every year?

C.J. think's I'm a nut, but San Francisco is really missing the boat. C.J. would make the perfect spokesperson. No one could ever be more passionate about San Francisco than he is.

06/20/06

My Dear Tina,

I truly hope today finds you well. Yesterday was a very good day for me. Diana and I slept in until 9AM, which is slightly unusual for us. We are normally early risers; up by 7AM, but we stayed up late the previous night and made up for it on the other side!

We prepared breakfast together, showered, and read the paper in bed. Then, as my custom, I went on-line and we listened to our favorite radio broadcast. Between the hours of 11AM and 1 PM (PST) there is a broadcast out of Everett WA that plays the best rock 'n' roll out there! A very old friend of mine is the DJ and both Diana and I love this station. Have I mentioned previously that we have a tremendous love for music? I do believe I have!

Sunday is our favorite day. Unless there's been a tragedy such as a death or a need to rush to the hospital, we never leave home on Sunday. Diana and I still enjoy the simple things in life; that has never changed. Some may think we live a boring life, but we believe our life together has been filled with more love and excitement than the norm.

You may be wondering if Diana and I still enjoy an active sex life. Of course, you may not be wondering that, but if I'm going to tell you the story I need to tell the complete story.

All marriages have their ups and downs. All couples go through, shall we say, dry spells? I cannot say that Diana and I have ever experienced that. Maybe we're unique. Maybe our marriage is unique. Maybe, just maybe, we have never allowed anything or anyone to ever come between us or the love that we share. We have always, and I mean always, put each other first. This is a lesson that

I'm proud to say we have passed on to our children. We have always believed that in order for us to raise healthy, loving children, we must nourish our relationship first and foremost. We have done that well.

Diana and I continue to enjoy a full sex life. We still look at each other and have the need to satisfy the others desires.

As we listened to our favorite station yesterday Diana and I made love. It never fails to amaze me, that although we are no longer in our twenties, our desire has never waned. The softness of her skin, the smell of her hair, the look of love in her eyes...this is what has made my life worth living.

Reading that letter again takes me back to the day that I received it. WOW! This wasn't just a marriage. This was an honest to God, once in a lifetime, love affair! Could anyone ever love me with that much passion after forty years? Could I ever love someone else with that much passion after forty years? How many people ever really experience that much love and passion in their lifetimes? And, what lesson can we all learn from this?

After reading this letter I realized that C.J. had me hooked. All he needed to do was reel me in! I became obsessed with his story. The next letter couldn't come quickly enough. I was fascinated with their life and their past. I had an intense need to know everything, and I was thrilled that C.J. felt comfortable with me, someone that he didn't even know, to share these most intimate moments with.

It would be more than two months before I would hear from C.J. again.

Chapter 3
Winds of Change

08/29/06

My Dearest Tina,

I am sending you my deepest regrets. I have not been communicating with you as I had promised, and have failed to reply to your e-mail messages. I fully understand your concern, and I could not feel worse than I do for letting this much time pass between my letters. To offer an explanation at this point would prove futile, so if it's okay with you I will just pick up where I left off.

Although Diana and I lived a life that many only dream of, we too had our moments. Our first fight actually took place on Alcatraz.

Diana and I had been married for six months and we were spending two weeks at Alcatraz. Jake and Sandra had left the island to vacation in Seattle, where their oldest daughter now lived. Diana and I were staying at Alcatraz to watch over the island.

It was our third night on the island and we were beginning to become a bit stir crazy. It was raining very hard and extremely cold outside. Diana heard a noise around 11:30 PM and decided that I should go investigate. I got out of bed and made my rounds throughout the house. Needless to say, I found nothing. After returning to the bedroom Diana informed me that the noise, she believed, was coming from outside the house, and I should go investigate. I was not willing to go outside in the cold and rain only to discover that it was a tree limb brushing against the house or perhaps a bird.

Now, I love my wife; I loved her then and I love her now. However, at that moment I saw a person that I didn't know. Diana jumped out of bed, grabbed her bathrobe, shoved her feet in her slippers, grabbed a flashlight and said

"Fine. I guess I'll be the man tonight." Well, do whatever you want to do. I smugly returned to the warm bed that I was so rudely asked to leave and then guilt set in. What was I doing? What if someone was out there? What if something happened to her? So, I jumped back out of bed and headed towards the door, which Diana had left wide open. The rain was coming down sideways and the floor was soaked. I felt myself losing my balance, but there was nothing I could do to stop the fall. Bam, straight down on my back. As I attempted to get back up Diana entered the house. She was soaked to the bone, took one look at me, and said "Don't bother coming now!"

Tina, I saw red! I regained my composure and back to the bedroom I went. Diana had disrobed and was standing next to the bed, drying herself with a towel. She took one look at me and in no uncertain terms told me exactly what she thought of me. I was no man, because no real man would allow their wife to venture outside in the middle of the night, in the pouring rain and in the cold to determine whether or not someone was on the property.

I walked over to my side of the bed, gave her one good, long look and replied "Fuck You!"

Diana literally jumped on the bed and as my mind raced wondering what this petite woman was about to do to me, she erupted in laughter.

As I lay there, flat on my back, Diana placed her body on top of mine. She took my hands in hers and pulled them up to the pillow that my head was resting on. She slowly moved on top of me and we made love until the wee hours of the morning.

Once again I knew I was at home with Diana and at home at Alcatraz. As you may have noticed, I am writing this to

Tina Westbrook

you today, August 29, the date Diana and I were married. I promise to you Tina, I will not stay gone long!

~ C.J

After a week had passed and I hadn't received a letter from C.J. I became concerned. This was so unlike him. So out of character. I immediately went to his profile on Classmates and found that he was still there, but had not posted any messages on his bulletin board. I sent him e-mails, not only to his Classmates address, but to his personal address as well. Another week had passed and still no word.

What happened to him? Did I do or say something that made him turn away? Was something wrong?

I began to worry that he may have become ill, or possibly Diana. Another week passed and I decided to contact some of his other friends on Classmates. *Perhaps they had news.*

Not a word from C.J. and no one seemed to know where he was or what was going on. I tried to calm my fears by telling myself that perhaps he and Diana had went away on vacation. They would be back soon I thought.

Yet another week passed by and still no word. I now began to think that C. J. was not on vacation. Something was not right, and there was no way for me to find out.

On August 29th I was thrilled to find a letter from C.J., but I was also concerned.

I read that letter and it seemed like C.J. was back. Telling his stories of Alcatraz and Diana, but I wasn't completely confident in what I should say.

I questioned myself over and over. *Do I ask him where he was? What happened? Or should I just forget that he had disappeared? After all, I reasoned, he will tell me if he wants me to know.* And with that I let it go. C. J. was apologetic. He knew I had been concerned. It wasn't my place or my right to question this man whom had shared so much. I knew what I needed to know. He was okay. Diana was okay. If he wanted to take a two month leave of absence then that was his right.

I did, however, notice there seemed to be a change in the tone of CJ.'s letters. I couldn't put my finger on it then, but something had most definitely changed. His letters seemed to be more defiant. I think that's a good word to describe them. He somehow didn't seem as "polite" in his writings as he previously had been. C.J. now began to use words that he had never used before. His letters had an underlying tone to them. Yes, defiant is a good word to use.

09/10/06

Hello Friend!

First and foremost, let me say HAPPY BIRTHDAY! Here's hoping that today is filled with much joy! My gift to you is the story of the day my son was born.

The date was October 3, 1970. Diana and I had been married for a little more than 3 years. We were filled with anticipation and excitement as we prepared for the birth of our first child. We did not know if we would be bringing a son or a daughter home, but we were prepared for either.

It was shortly after 12 O'clock noon when I received a call at work. It was Jake. Diana was in labor and they were on their way to the hospital. Jake and Sandra had been staying with us at our home for two weeks. Sandra had been worried that Diana would go into labor early, so they had friends watch over Alcatraz.

The moment I received the call I made a dash out the door. I later was told that I never said a word and took off as if the building were on fire.

Traffic was horrendous and it took me a full hour to get to the hospital, which was only 16 miles away.

When I arrived Diana was already in the delivery room, and I was not permitted to go back there. I found Jake and Sandra and we did what several others were doing; we waited.

Shortly after 2pm a nurse appeared and told me that I had a son. A 5lb 8 oz son. She went on to explain that we could see the baby and Diana shortly.

Tina, as God as my witness, I had never been so overcome with pure joy. Tears filled my eyes and quickly streamed down my face. I was so happy! I wish I could say that this was the happiest day of my life, but I would be lying. The happiest day of my life was the day I married my son's mother. Nothing could ever compare to that, but this was a very close second!

The moment I held my son in my arms I changed. From that moment on I knew I was responsible for insuring he grow into a good man. I knew I was not raising a boy, but rather a man. Both Diana and I took that role very seriously. He would know right from wrong. He would understand the meaning of love and respect. And, if I ever taught him anything, he would know that women were to be placed on a pedestal. For what are we without women?

That letter was truly one of the best birthday gifts I have ever received. For a man to express his feelings about the day he became a father so eloquently and without fear of appearing "sensitive" was something that many of us rarely experience.

I do not understand why we, as a society, teach our sons that it's somehow wrong to express their feelings; that expressing how they feel makes them "less of a man". C.J. has taught me that being true to who you are is what's important. He once told me "To leave this world having not expressed how you feel is sad, but to live in this world and not express how you feel is a tragedy."

C.J. must have made his parents proud and I have no doubt that his son has made both he and Diana proud.

"Please prepare for landing." *What? I l*ooked over at Chuck as he was putting his tray table back in place.

"Wow, we're here?" I asked.

"Yeah, you've been so absorbed in those letters that I wondered if you'd even realize the plane had landed and everyone was gone!"

I let out a laugh and Mr. Window seat joined in the chit chat. "So, you ready to meet your pen pal?"

I smiled at Mr. Window seat and let my heart do the talking. "I've already met my pen pal, and I can't wait to see him!"

As we sat in our seats waiting for the okay to unfasten our seat belts Chuck placed his hand on mine. "Hey Tina, here's my phone number. Just in case. I'll be right over in Oakland. It wouldn't take me long to get to San Francisco. Call me if anything goes wrong. Okay?"

I was touched by his sincerity and I wanted him to know that. "Chuck, I'm sure everything's going to be just fine. You're very sweet. Thank you."

Chuck looked me directly in my eyes and said "Well, I don't know about being sweet, but I kinda feel like someone should be looking out for you. Just know you have a friend in California!" I smiled and thought to myself *I have two friends in California!*

We exited the airplane and as we made our way through the terminal Mr. Window seat spoke up. "Well, this is it. I didn't check any luggage, so I'm outta here. Good luck with your pen pal!"

Chuck and I both smiled and before I knew it Mr. Window seat shook Chuck's hand and wrapped his arms around me. He whispered into my ear "Remember...meet him in a public place!" *It was Mr. Window seat that had said that!* I laughed and assured him that I would.

"Hey, by the way, what's your name?" Mr. Window seat smiled and replied "My name is Tony. Tony Richter. I'm a San Francisco Homicide Detective, and I don't want you to be my next call." Chills ran down my spine.

I retrieved my luggage from baggage claim and went outside to find my shuttle bus. The airport was bustling and after nearly ten minutes I found where I needed to be. I boarded the shuttle and took a seat directly behind the driver.

"Hello! Is this your first trip to San Francisco?" I smiled politely at the driver and explained to him that this was not my first visit to San Francisco, but that it had been a while since my last visit. The driver smiled back at me and then pulled the van onto the road.

"Wow, traffic is really backed up, isn't it?"

The driver looked at me through his rear view mirror and replied "Yes. This is normal though for this time of the day. I hope you're not in a hurry!" The driver chuckled a bit and went on to explain that every day, no matter what time of the day it is, is busy. "That's one of the things ya gotta love about San Francisco! Never a dull moment! People everywhere! This city never rests!"

I thought about that and wondered if this guy was after C. J.'s job as spokesman for the Chamber of Commerce.

I had reservations at the Fisherman's Wharf Marriott and had been told that it was a short twenty minute commute. I'm sure that would have been correct providing there had been no other vehicles on the road. The short twenty minute commute actually resulted in a forty-five minute commute.

As I entered the hotel I quickly glanced around. I found my surroundings to be quite pleasant. A comfortable place, I thought to myself. The lobby was quite spacious and the floors shined. I noticed several oversized leather chairs and a fireplace. My eyes quickly darted towards the bar. Yes, I could see myself sitting over there with a glass of wine in my hand. Very nice I thought.

"Hello! Welcome to the Marriott! Will you be checking in?" The young lady behind the desk seemed to be very happy being there. She had long, blonde hair, beautiful eyes and a smile that lit up the room.

I smiled back at her, noticing her name on the tag that was attached to her blouse, and replied "Yes, I am. Tina Westbrook."

"Hello Ms. Westbrook. One moment please."

After entering my name into her computer she opened a drawer and removed an electronic key. I will send someone up with your luggage shortly. You will be staying in room 506, that's a king guestroom". She handed me the key and motioned toward the elevator.

"Is there anything else that I can do for you?" she asked.

"No, Katie, thank you."

Katie smiled and then told me to have a nice day and enjoy my stay.

I took the elevator up to the fifth floor and entered my room. *So, lets see what the Marriott in San Francisco has to offer.* I walked in, threw my purse and file folder down, and took inventory.

Very nice...king sized bed, wouldn't mind hitting that right now! Oh, full size desk, and oh yeah...high speed internet! All the comforts of home! Including a 32 inch LCD HDTV! Good deal! I ventured into the bathroom and again found myself very pleased. *Okay...look at that elegant lighting. Simply beautiful! And granite?! Yes! This is my kind of place!*

I quietly congratulated myself on such a good choice of hotel and realized that I was very hungry. One quick look at my watch and I understood why. It was now after 2pm my time, and it was definitely lunch time here in sunny California. Time for some room service.

I found the room service menu and picked up the telephone. After placing my order I was informed that it would be forty minutes. *No problem. I'll just take a hot bath, put on some comfy clothes, and make myself at home.*

Nearly twenty minutes had passed and as I made my way from the bathroom toward the desk I was startled by the ringing of the telephone.

Oh great...they probably don't have what I ordered! I answered the telephone expecting to hear someone from room service apologizing, but immediately after answering the phone I realized that it was not room service, but C. J.

"Tina! Welcome to San Francisco!" C.J. sounded exuberant!

"C.J. Hello! I can't believe I'm finally hearing your voice!" This was the first time C.J. and I had ever spoken to each other. All of our communication during the past year had only been through e-mail.

"Well, believe it! How was your flight? Non eventful I'm hoping."

"The flight was good. I sat between a San Francisco Homicide detective and a gentleman from Atlanta. They were both very... well, lets just say they were very interesting!"

C.J. chuckled and replied "Well, most people have to wait until they actually arrive in San Francisco to meet *interesting* people! You were lucky!"

I suddenly realized that C.J. was quite the character and had a fantastic sense of humor.

"Oh no...C.J., I'm sorry...can you hold the phone for a second? I ordered a bite for lunch and they're at the door."

"Oh, hey, that's okay. I just wanted to make sure that you arrived and all was good. Enjoy your lunch, get some rest and we'll talk tomorrow. Sound good?"

"Sounds great! It was nice talking to you C.J. Have a wonderful evening!"

"You too my dear! Talk tomorrow! Bye!" And that was it. My first conversation with C.J. As I opened the door for room service I thought to myself that C.J. had sounded exactly as I had imagined.

After consuming every bite of my lunch I grabbed the file folder with C.J.'s letters, turned on the television, and made myself comfortable on the king sized bed.

09/21/06

Dear Tina

I hope today finds you well. I have given much thought to today's letter and have decided to tell you a bit about Richard Oakes, or as the press liked to call him, "The Mayor of Alcatraz."

Tragedy struck Alcatraz during the early part of 1970. Oakes had a young step-daughter; I believe her name to be Yvonne. I have heard different reports regarding this child's age. Some say she was twelve years old, some say she was thirteen. Regardless of her age, she suffered a tremendous fall on the island. The events of this tragedy have also been told with different versions. Some simply say that Yvonne was killed in a fall on the island, while others, including Sandra, say that she fell from three flights of stairs falling onto the concrete floor. What we do know is that Sandra was one of the first people to come to the child's aid. Yvonne died the day following her fall from massive head injuries.

When Jake and Sandra finally decided to leave Alcatraz it couldn't have been a moment too soon.

The destruction was down right ugly. The Indians had stripped every piece of wood they could find from the buildings, and had used it for heat during the cool nights.

There was no water in any of the buildings, resulting in no flushable toilets. The Indians had excremented in every un-flushable toilet that was available.

Sadly, they had burned down the doctors house. It was complete and utter pandemonium and destruction. In addition to burning down the doctors house, they torched the wardens beautiful home. I had been in this home several times and it was just beautiful! The house sat on top of a hill overlooking a 360 degree perimeter of the gorgeous San Francisco Bay. The only thing left standing to remind us of what had been and what it now had become was a concrete wall.

Even as I write this to you my stomach wrenches and my heart aches, nearly bringing me to tears For the Indians, this was a conquest. A point to prove. For me and my family, this was an attack on the land and place that we dearly loved.

This was Alcatraz.

It was on November 9, 1969 when Richard Oakes and a group of Indian supporters chartered a boat, the Monte Cristo, and headed out to symbolically claim Alcatraz Island. It was on November 20, 1969 that their symbolic occupation turned into a full scale occupation that would last until June 11, 1971.

There were a total of three separate occupations of Alcatraz Island. The first was actually on March 9, 1964, the second on November 9, 1969 and the third, which would last nineteen months, on November 20, 1969.

The 1964 occupation was carried out by five Sioux Indians, led by Richard McKenzie. The Indians demanded the use of the island for a cultural center and an Indian University.

Richard Oakes planned the November 9, 1969 occupation along with a group of Indian students and a group of urban Indians from the Bay Area. During a meeting following the November 9th occupation, Oakes and his fellow American Indian students realized that a long term occupation was possible. Oakes recruited Indian students during a visit to the American Indian Studies Center at UCLA.

Once the occupiers had established themselves on the island, organization began. An elected council was put into place and everyone on the island had a job.

The Federal Government insisted that the Indians leave the island and they placed an ineffective barricade around the island. The government, however, did agree to the Indians demands that formal negotiations be held. The Indians wanted the deed to the island, they wanted to establish an Indian University, a cultural center and a museum. The government negotiators refused the Indians demands and insisted that they leave the island.

By early 1970 the Indian organization began to fall apart. During the month of January the Indian students began returning to school. The students were replaced by Indian people from the urban areas and from reservations who had not been involved during the initial occupation. In addition, many non Indians began taking up residency on the island; including many from the San Francisco hippie and drug culture. On January 5, 1970, Oakes thirteen year old stepdaughter fell three floors down a stairwell to her death. Soon after that tragedy Oakes left the island.

The federal government responded to the occupation by adopting a position of noninterference and the FBI was directed to remain clear of the island. In addition, the Coast Guard was directed not to interfere and the Government Services Administration, also known as the GSA, was instructed not to remove the Indians from Alcatraz Island. The Indians believed that negotiations were finally taking place, but the federal government was playing a waiting game. The government offered the Indians a portion of Fort Miley in San Francisco, but the Indians refused and it became clear that the Indians would take nothing less than full title to Alcatraz Island.

The government retaliated by shutting off all electrical power. They also removed the water barge which had provided fresh water to the island. Three days after the water barge had been removed a fire broke out on the island and several historic buildings were destroyed.

As time passed, the problems on the island only worsened. Daily reports from the government caretaker on the island told of the open use of drugs, and a general disarray of leadership.

By 1971 the Indian occupiers began stripping copper wiring and copper tubing from the buildings and selling it as scrap metal. Three of the Indian occupiers were arrested, tried and found guilty. It was also at this time that the press turned against the Indians and began publishing stories of beatings and assaults.

It was in January 1971, after two oil tankers collided in the entrance to the San Francisco Bay, that the federal government took action. President Nixon gave the approval to remove the occupants from the island. However, it was to be done when the smallest number of people were on the island, and they were instructed to use as little force as possible.

On June 10, 1971 armed federal marshals, FBI agents and special forces swarmed the island and removed five women, four children and six unarmed Indian men.

It would seem that the Indians had lost their battle for Alcatraz Island, but in reality, they were able to acquire their original demands; with the exception of the full title to Alcatraz Island. President Nixon returned Blue Lake and 48,000 acres of land to the Taos Indians. Occupied lands near Davis California would become home to a Native American university and it lead to the hiring of Native American's to work in the federal agency that had such an impact on their lives.

10/01/06

Compliments to you my dear! The new photos that you have posted are spectacular! Once again you have given all of us a new way to see Niagra Falls! Kudos!

I thought today that I would share with you what life was like in San Francisco during the 1960's.

One of my most vivid memories of that time actually took place in January 1966. The hippie movement was well underway and several of my friends had jumped right on the "Love Train!" Myself included! I am not proud of all that I have done in my life, but there are some things that I believed in then, and still do today.

In January 1966 I would find myself at San Francisco's Longshoreman's Hall. I was there, along with numerous friends, to attend an event that was referred to as "The Trips Festival". Ten thousand people attended this sold out event, which lasted three days, and more than a thousand were turned away each night. The event took place on a Friday, Saturday and Sunday. I was there on Saturday night. That night the Grateful Dead and Big Brother and the Holding Company were on stage. We were there for the music, yes, but we were also there to witness the first fully developed light show. Tina, this would be one of those moments in time, that if I could, I would go back and change completely. I never would have went to this event, and if I did go, I would have given more thought to my actions. For, it was on this night, along with six thousand other people, that I willingly used LSD. I really had no idea what I was getting my self into, because I really knew nothing about LSD. Thinking back to that time, I'm not really sure I had ever heard of LSD. Nonetheless, it was openly available at the concert; in disguise as punch.

It would be more than eight months later that California would declare LSD a controlled substance, which made the drug illegal. However, by that time a lot of us had already used LSD and had made it a part of our lives. I was one of those people.

By the time that I met Diana, in August of 1966, I had been using LSD for more than six months; actually seven months. I was a hippie. Although I made a point to maintain a "normal" lifestyle; normal job, normal friends (for the most part) and a normal relationship with my family, there was that part of me that enjoyed new experiences, and I fully and completely believed in the hippie way of life.

Music has always been my passion, and music played a very large part within the hippie culture. There were endless nights of music, dancing, and drugs. By the beginning of summer 1966 several bands had moved to the Haight-Ashbury neighborhood, including Jefferson Airplane and the Grateful Dead. It was an unforgettable time, which I remember with great joy as well as great regret.

During this period more than 15,000 hippies had moved into San Francisco and I began to live my life without boundaries. I had sex with young ladies that I didn't know, and didn't care to know. Names, forget it! It was a time of free love, peace and personal freedom. I had bought into this lifestyle, but all the while trying to maintain my life as the perfect son, the perfect employee, the straight laced kid from San Francisco.

This was San Francisco in 1966. This was my life in San Francisco in 1966. I was unaware of the direction my life was about to take. I thought I knew who I was and what I stood for, but within a years time I would realize that I knew nothing. I would learn that for every action there is a reaction, and I would learn that we must all stand up and take responsibility for our actions. I would soon learn what it meant to be a man.

10/09/06

Hello My Friend! Here's hoping all is well! I am going to continue where I left off last time...

By the end of August, 1966 I had met Diana, and although she was quite open and easy to talk to, I had chosen to hide my drug use. I told myself that it was not a problem, and there was no need to discuss it with her because I didn't know her all that well, and I didn't want to chance losing her. Again, I found myself leading two separate lives.

During January 1967 Diana attended the Human-Be-In, which was organized by Michael Bowen. Diana went with some of her girlfriends from school and I stayed behind. I wanted to attend, but the fear of running into people who knew who and what I was kept me away. More than 20,000 hippies attended the gathering, which took place at Golden Gate Park. Diana's reason for going was pure and simple curiosity. She had an interest in learning as much as she could about people and different ways of life. Little did she know that she was dating someone that indulged completely in what she was trying to learn about.

So, as fate would have it, while Diana attended the rally, I decided to head over to a friends house. My one and only reason for going there that day was to get high. I entered the apartment, which was a very large Victorian, beautiful really, and as usual it was jam packed with bodies. To this day I could not tell you how many people actually lived in that apartment. I made my way over to my friend Rick and we went into the kitchen where he offered up a cold beer. We made ourselves comfortable at the table, drank our beer and we both took a hit of LSD.

Rick and I had just begun to talk about the event that was taking place at Golden Gate Park when a very pretty, very young, and very pregnant girl peeked from around the corner. I smiled politely and just as I was about to say hello I recognized her. She must have noticed the look of recognition on my face because she walked over to me, looked me directly in my eyes and asked me what I was going to do about her situation. What was I going to do about her situation? This girl was pointing the finger at me!

I attempted to laugh it off and dismiss her, but she continued to get in my face. She point blank informed me that she didn't sleep around and one way or the other I was going to pay for this.

Tina, I'm usually a very peaceful person. I would never harm anyone, but at that moment I snapped. That's the only way to describe what happened next.

I grabbed her arm and told her that I wasn't about to own up to something that I wasn't for sure I was responsible for. That didn't sit too well with her because with her free hand she came across and smacked me in the face. All the while screaming that she didn't sleep around.

I pushed her away from me and started to head out of the room when I felt a blow to my back. I slightly lost my footing and when I looked back at her I noticed that she had a frying pan in her hand. Rick moved past me and I moved towards her. I grabbed the frying pan from her hand and pushed her again; this time I pushed too hard and she fell through an open window. As I realized what was happening, it was too late. She fell from the second floor and her body crashed against the sidewalk below.

Rick and I ran through the apartment, out the front door, down the stairs and onto the street. A large crowd had already formed and people were screaming "Call the police, call an ambulance!" As I looked over at this young girl I knew instantly that she was dead. People were asking what happened and I couldn't move. I couldn't speak. I just stood there looking at this young girl dead on the sidewalk. I began to shake uncontrollably.

Rick put his hand on my shoulder and whispered into my ear "We don't know nothing. We were walking out of the kitchen and she fell, or jumped. We're not sure what happened."

The police arrived shortly after the ambulance. Looking back on it now it seems like a bad dream. They were firing questions off and wanted to know who this girl was, what was her name, how did this happen, and what was our connection to the girl. Both Rick and I shook our heads. We didn't know nothing. The girl had started staying at the house a few weeks earlier. Rick only knew her as Sam. Maybe someone else in the house would know more. Then they asked who the father of the baby was. Again, Rick and I didn't know nothing. The police went upstairs to question the other housemates and Rick and I left.

When we arrived at my house I was still shaking. I felt responsible for what happened to that girl; Sam. Rick told me not to worry about it, that it wasn't my fault, but I knew it was. Rick didn't see it. I pushed her and she fell out the window. I killed Sam and her unborn baby. Rick promised me that he would never say a word to anyone about what happened and I believed him, but would I be able to live with myself? I had that answer in a week.

10/13/06

Hi Tina,

After Rick left my house that fateful evening I had an overwhelming desire to go to the police station and confess that I had killed Sam. I smoked some marijuana, trying to calm myself down, while reminding myself that turning myself in would only destroy my future. There was nothing that was going to bring Sam back and knowing what I had done would kill my parents.

I paced the house for hours and then decided to go for a long walk. As I wandered the streets of San Francisco I found myself right back where it had all happened. I was standing in front of Ricks apartment building. I stood there, glaring at that sidewalk, until I heard someone call my name. When I turned to face the apartment building I saw Mike, an old friend of mine.

Mike asked me if I had heard what had happened earlier that day. I told him that I knew what happened because I had been there visiting Rick. He started to ask more questions; Did I see it happen? How did it happen? Who was she? I told Mike exactly what Rick and I had rehearsed and I followed Mike upstairs to Ricks apartment.

As we entered the apartment Rick looked over at me and appeared to be concerned. We said hello to each other and then Rick said he had something to show me, so we walked into a bedroom. Rick closed the door and began to tell me what he had found out since returning back to the apartment.

Sam had come to San Francisco back in March 1966. She was only 16 years old when she ran away from home. Home had been Arkansas. Just like so many other people at that time, she had heard about the life in San Francisco, the music, the peace, the personal freedom. She was attracted to the dream that so many young people left home for to find.

Another girl, Kelly, who had also been staying at Ricks apartment, met Sam shortly after she arrived in San Francisco. Kelly, who was a few years older than Sam, took Sam under her wing and looked after her like a younger sister

Kelly told Rick that Sam had discovered she was pregnant in May. She had only slept with one guy since she had arrived in San Francisco, and she had met that guy at a get together one night at Golden Gate Park.

Rick then asked me if I remembered being there and meeting Sam. I explained that Sam looked familiar to me, but I wasn't able to place her. He went on to tell me that the get together that Kelly had been talking about was a free for all, drug induced, sex party.

I thought my head was going to explode. Yes, I remembered being there. Now I remember Sam. I had been smoking pot for hours, drinking alcohol in excess, and I had also taken a hit of LSD that evening. I remember it being very late in the evening, possibly after midnight, when I spotted Sam. I had already indulged in sex with two other women that evening and I was pretty messed up. I don't remember who approached who, but I do remember having sex with her. I was 23 years old and I had sex with a 16 year old. As these memories came flooding back I found myself becoming ill. Then the realization that Sam had not been lying, that she was pregnant with my child, hit me like a brick. I had not only caused the death of this very young girl, but I had killed my own child.

Suddenly I couldn't breathe and I told Rick that I had to go. Rick reminded me to stay calm and not worry. The police had said that this was an apparent accident, and unless one of us did something stupid, it would remain an accident. I just had to stay cool.

I spoke with Diana a couple of times the days following Sam's death. Diana wanted to get together and tell me all about the Human-Be-In. She wanted to see me, because we had not spent our usual weekend together, but I kept putting her off. I was unable to sleep and I had called in sick to work for 2 days straight. I tried to tell Diana that I still wasn't feeling well and I was afraid she may catch whatever I had, but Diana wouldn't take no for an answer. She exclaimed that she was coming over and going to nurse me back to health.

I headed for the shower and I worried how I would react in front of Diana. Would it be obvious that I wasn't really sick? Would she instinctively know that something else was wrong? Would she be able to look at me and know I had killed someone? I decided that I would have to get rid of Diana as soon as possible. That's something I never thought I would hear myself say.

Diana arrived and the first thing out of my mouth was "I really don't think you should be here; I feel really bad." Diana placed her hand on my forehead and told me she didn't think I had a fever. I told her that "I may not have a fever, but I feel really bad." That didn't seem to make a difference to her. She walked over to the stereo system and turned on the radio.

She then headed towards the kitchen, and I followed her. I asked her what she was doing and she said that she was going to cook. I told her that I wasn't hungry, but she went on about her business. I walked out of the kitchen and told

58

her to do whatever she wanted to do. I walked back into the living room and threw myself into a chair.

Nearly 15 minutes had passed before I walked back into the kitchen. Diana was cooking like there was no tomorrow and I sat down at the table. She asked me if I wanted something to drink and I told her that she was just wasting her time. I wasn't hungry, I didn't feel well, and this probably wasn't a good idea.

Without saying a word Diana picked the pot up from the cook top, walked over to the garbage can, poured the contents into the garbage and left the kitchen. I followed her into the living room and she grabbed her purse and walked out the door. I called her name and asked her to wait a second, but she never responded. She just kept walking.

Three days later I found myself sitting at the San Francisco Police Department.

I will continue this story next week. Right now I must leave. I am going to visit my mother today; it's her 87th birthday.

10/20/06

Hello My Dear! I was hoping to continue where I left off before now, but life has been very busy this week.

I had not spoken to Diana in 3 days and I was worried that I had ran her off for good. She hadn't called me, but in all fairness, I had not called her either. I worried about Diana, I worried about Sam, and I worried about my future.

The days that followed Sam's death are a blur. I remember being panicked. I remember Rick telling me to say nothing, and I remember treating Diana terribly. But, the days just came and went. I was in a constant state of worry. I tried to go to work, but couldn't concentrate, and went home early. I spent that week pacing the floor and getting high. I soon realized that no matter how high I got I couldn't escape the feeling of doom.

Six days after Sam's untimely death I knew I had to do the right thing. For the first time in nearly a week I felt relief.

I took a long shower, put on a pair of my best khaki's and a blue oxford, and left my house; not knowing if I would be returning.

As I entered the police department I suddenly felt the urge to run. Just get out of there. What was I doing? They had no idea what had happened and I was about to give them a reason to lock me away for life. Just as I turned to walk back out I heard a voice from behind me asking if I needed help.

I turned to look at the person asking if I needed help and found a uniformed police officer standing in front of me. Right then and there I knew I needed to do the right thing because I couldn't live with myself otherwise. I told the officer that I needed to speak with a detective; that there had been a young girl killed a few days back, she had fallen out of a window, and landed on the sidewalk.

The officer told me to take a seat and he would send someone out. I waited for what seemed like a lifetime, but in all actuality, was 15 minutes.

A very tall, good looking man stepped out from behind a door and told me to come on back. I got up and followed him into a small room. The room was empty with the exception of a small table and two chairs. The man introduced himself as Detective Ingall and asked me how he could help me. I asked him if he knew about Sam, the young girl who had been killed when she fell out of a second story window.

Detective Ingall told me that he knew of the case and asked me what I needed. I took a deep breath and told him that I was there when she fell out the window. I told him that we had an argument and after she hit me with a frying pan I pushed her to get her away from me and she fell out the window. I told him that I was responsible for her death.

Detective Ingall sat there, looking at me as if I were crazy, and proceeded to tell me that it didn't matter how she fell out of the window. The case had been closed. Ruled an accident. He went on to tell me that she wasn't even from San Francisco, or California for that matter. She had been a hippie that ran away from home, got herself pregnant, and was a heavy drug user. The autopsy showed large amounts of marijuana and LSD in her system. Then he said something that I will never forget. He looked me directly in my eyes and said 'You know, you're a good kid, clean cut, you have your entire life ahead of you. Don't go worrying about some chick that messed up her life. People like her aren't worth worrying about."

Tina, it was in that very moment that I understood how this world operated. Unless you fit the stereotypical ideal of what a "good" person is, then society could care less about you.

If you were killed at the hands of another person it would only matter if you were what society deemed as "good." Otherwise, your death wouldn't matter. You would just be considered a burden taken off of society.

Sam's death meant nothing because of how she lived her life.

I thanked Detective Ingall for his time, shook his hand and walked out of that room. As I left the police department I turned back around, took a long look at that building, and vowed that I would live my life in a meaningful manner. I would not be one of those people that ended up dead, knowing that some ignorant detective would be telling my parents that my death didn't matter because I had drugs in my system, and basically deserved what I got.

After my meeting with Detective Ingall I walked over to Diana's apartment and sat down on the porch steps. I sat there for three hours; just watching people walk by. When Diana was in sight I stood up and walked towards her. She looked at me with both surprise and confusion and asked what I was doing there. I said all I knew to say. I told her that I loved her and I was sorry.

11/01/06

Dear Tina,

As the holidays approach, I'm wondering if I ever told you about my first Christmas with Diana? I don't believe I have, but if I'm wrong, please bare with me...I'm old! And, the story is worth telling, and hearing, twice!

Christmas 1966 was, without question, the best Christmas of my life.

Diana and I had been dating for nearly four months and as Christmas grew closer I was trying to decide what I should get for her. She hadn't dropped any hints, and try as I may, I could not get her to tell me what she wanted or needed. I would ask and she would just smile. So, in my desperation, I boarded a ferry and went to Alcatraz. If anyone knew what Diana wanted it would be Sandra.

Christmas was one week away and I didn't know what to do. I sat at the kitchen table explaining my predicament to Jake and Sandra, but they weren't exactly gushing with ideas. Finally, as my frustration climbed to an all new level, I point blank asked them what I should do? Jake laughed and Sandra shrugged her shoulders. I sat there drowning in self pity and it must have been obvious because Jake finally decided to throw me a rope.

That evening Diana and I were at our favorite Italian restaurant when she asked me about family plans for Christmas. I explained to her that I needed to be at my parents on Christmas Eve; family tradition. We all gathered at mom and dad's on Christmas Eve; grandparents, aunts, uncles, cousins. Big Italian Family. There was no way out of that, but she was welcome to join us.

Diana looked disappointed and told me that she would be spending Christmas at Alcatraz with her family. Well, I surmised, I guess we should spend the day before Christmas Eve together, and that's what we did.

Diana had been staying at my house since school broke for the holidays. It was the day before Christmas Eve and as Diana slept in I crept into the kitchen and prepared her favorite breakfast. Pancakes, bacon, eggs and orange juice. I placed her breakfast on a plate and then put the plate on a serving tray and headed into the bedroom.

As I entered the bedroom Diana was sitting up in bed. She smiled and told me that she thought she smelled something good cooking. I smiled back at her, kissed her, and placed the tray on her lap. I then headed out the bedroom door.

Diana asked me where I was going and I told her that I would be right back.

I eased my way through the living room and reached for a small box that I had hidden inside the little Christmas tree that Diana had put up.

I returned to the bedroom and I had my hand behind my back. Diana looked up at me and asked me what I was doing. I walked over to her and placed the little box on the serving tray. Diana smiled and asked me if she could open it. I gave her the go ahead and she grabbed that little box with more excitement than I had ever seen a child exhibit on Christmas morning.

Diana unwrapped the box and when she lifted the lid off of it her mouth flew open and tears ran down her face.

Inside that tiny box were the words that I had wanted to say to Diana, but never quite got them out. A silver, heart shaped locket said it for me. Engraved on the front of the locket was "I Love You."

Diana looked at me with tears running down her face and quietly whispered "I love you too!" We spent the rest of the morning making love.

Talk soon my dear ~ C.J

11/10/06

Hello Tina My Dear,

I hope everything is going well for you. I will continue my first Christmas story with Diana for you.

It was the afternoon before Christmas Eve and I walked with Diana to the docks so she could board a ferry to the island. The last ferry would leave at 6PM and she didn't want to take any chances, so after spending the morning making love, she decided to leave.

It was very cold that day and Diana was bundled up in her favorite jacket, scarf around her neck and her blue jeans were tucked inside her knee high boots. She was truly a vision.

We kissed goodbye, Diana boarded the ferry, and I walked home alone.

It was 6PM that evening as I approached the docks again. I boarded a ferry and with much anticipation, I was on my way to Alcatraz. As the ferry moved closer to the island I began to imagine how Diana would react as she realized that I had forgone my original Christmas plans and traditions, to be with her.

I arrived at Alcatraz Island and as I exited the ferry I spotted Jake. We shook hands, and made our way to his house.

Instead of walking directly in, we knocked on the door and inside the house Sandra instructed Diana to answer the door.

The door swung open and Diana screamed with delight. She threw her arms around me and kissed me as if she hadn't seen me in years.

Jake had been right that day I paid him and Sandra a visit trying to determine what I should give Diana for Christmas. Jake had thrown a drowning fool in love a rope and he was right on the money. He already knew then what I didn't know; Diana was in love with me and her only wish for Christmas was that we could be together.

We spent the next three days creating new Christmas traditions and memories that would last a lifetime. Traditions that we would pass on to our children. We didn't know it then, but this would be the first of 40 Christmases that we would spend together.

Happy Holidays Dear ~ C. J.

12/01/06

My Dear Tina,

Hope this finds you well. Christmas is less than 3 weeks away and I am still running around in an attempt to finish my shopping, but no worry, I will get it all done!

This time of year often finds me thinking of Jake. He was such a wonderful man and I miss him terribly. Jake was not the father in law that most young men hate to end up with. Jake was warm and friendly, and he always knew what to do and what to say; even when I didn't. I loved my own father, and I miss him as much as I miss Jake, but Jake seemed to understand me. More than anyone else. He once told me that when he looked at me he saw himself all too often. Perhaps he took pity on me! If that were the case he never let it be known.

Jake worked as a prison guard from 1941 to 1963. Jake was a well liked man and respected by other guards, as well as the prisoners. Jake and his family, along with twenty other families, knew Alcatraz as their home. It was during a 1946 jail break that two guards were murdered. Shortly after that incident Jake transferred from Levenworth Federal Prison to Alcatraz.

As one may imagine, this was quite the change for Sandra and the children. Their lives were forever changed with that move to Alcatraz. The children would wake every morning, get ready for school, and take a water taxi to San Francisco, where they attended school.

Diana was only 1 year old when her family moved to Alcatraz, so all of her memories growing up took place with Alcatraz prison as the back drop. Living on the island seemed normal to Diana. This was the only life she had ever known, and I remember the day that I fully understood that.

Diana and I were at the Marina Safeway, a grocery store that was in San Francisco, near the boat dock. As Diana and I waited for the cashier to finish ringing up our items a conversation broke out between the two of them. The cashier asked Diana what our plans for the weekend were. Diana replied that we were going to the island. The cashier then paused for a moment and replied "Oh! You're going to Hawaii?" Diana stood there with a look of confusion and then with a slight smile she answered "No. Alcatraz Island."

My memories are very clear regarding Alcatraz, and I fondly remember the time I spent there. ~ C.J.

12/09/06

Hello Tina! Hope today finds you well. I ran into an old acquaintance this afternoon, which was rather odd. I had not seen him since 1969; nearly 40 years ago! At first I didn't even recognize him, but he was staring at me so I approached him. I asked him if we knew each other and he laughed and was surprised that I didn't remember him. Then he said "How could you not remember me? We worked together for more than 5 years!"

I took a good look at him and realized it was Billy. I'm not sure if I've ever told you about Billy; I doubt I have since he was one of those skeletons in my closet that I wish would just stay there. But, there he was, standing right in front of me. After a bit of small talk we shook hands and went our separate ways. I'm mentioning this to you because Billy played a small, but significant role in my life. And, if I'm going to tell you my story, I need to tell the entire story.

I met Billy in 1964. I was 21 years of age and Billy was a year my senior. We were both working at my fathers car dealership. Billy and I didn't get along because he assumed that I had it made around there; being the owners son. Then one day I made a tremendous mistake and became indebted to Billy.

I had been driving one of the cars to and from home for about a week because my personal car was being repaired in the body shop; a small fender bender. The day my car was ready Billy came walking into my office and told me that he was going to drive the car that I had been using back to the service department to have it cleaned up. I told Billy that I would take it back there in a little while and Billy said okay. I thought that was the end of that.

It was nearly lunch time and I walked outside to remove my personal items from the car that I had been driving, only to find the car gone. My heart began to race and I immediately began to sweat. I ran back inside and asked Katherine, the secretary, where the car was. Katherine informed me that Billy drove it back to the service department.

I went flying back to the service department and found Billy standing next to the car. I walked over to him and asked him why he brought the car back there. I had told him I would do it. Billy had a smirk on his face, placed his hand on my shoulder and suggested we walk outside for a moment.

Once outside Billy told me that he knew I wasn't the upstanding fine young man that I led everyone to believe I was, and now I was going to have to do him a favor. In return, he would keep my secret.

I started to walk away when Billy grabbed my arm and told me that he had some of my personal belongings and unless I wanted him to give them to my father I had better listen up.

I asked Billy what he wanted and he told me that he wanted me to drive over to Oakland that night and pick up a package. Then he wanted me to bring the package to him. Once I did that, he in turn, would hand over my belongings and not tell my father what he had found.

That night I made the drive to Oakland. Per Billy's instructions, I arrived at exactly 9PM. I pulled into the parking lot of a local motel, backed my car into the parking space in front of room number 104, killed the lights, got out of the car and opened the trunk, then got back inside the car and waited.

The entire time I was not believing that I was actually doing this. Billy had me between a rock and a hard place and all I could think about was taking a gun to that son of a bitches head and splattering his brains across the dealership.

I sat in that parking lot for what seemed to be forever, but in reality, was only 20 minutes. In the rear view mirror I saw 2 men walk out of room 104, raise the opened trunk, places boxes inside the trunk, and then slam it shut. The 2 men walked back into the motel room and I left the parking lot.

I couldn't wait to get back to San Francisco. I was a nervous wreck and I wanted any and all dealings with Billy to be done with.

As I drove my car onto the lot at the dealership I noticed Billy and another guy waiting by the side of the building. I turned the car off, killed the lights and stepped out of the car. Billy was telling me to hurry and open the trunk, which I did. Billy and his cohort grabbed up the boxes and placed them in the trunk of their car. Billy slammed the trunk closed and then walked up to me with a paper bag. I opened the bag and discovered my belongings. 2 baggies filled with marijuana, that I had just picked up that morning, along with 2 bottles of pills.

Billy slapped me on the back and told me it was nice doing business with me. He then walked toward his partner', pulled a gun and shot him dead.

I just stood there frozen in my tracks and then instinct told me to get out of there. Before I could get my car door open I felt Billy's hand on my back.

Billy told me to get in my car and keep my mouth shut. If I said a word to anyone about what had happened then the 2 gentleman that were at the motel would put a bullet in my head. Then Billy smiled and said "I think we're going to get along just fine."

Billy got in his car and left. I took a good, long look at the body lying dead in the lot of my fathers dealership. For a moment I considered going inside and calling the police, but instead, I jumped in my car and drove home.

It was 6:30 the next morning when I received a phone call from my father. He was very upset and told me that the lot would be closed that day because a body had been found shot to death next to the service department. The police were there and they were investigating. They thought it had been a drug deal gone bad. Some poor loser had gotten himself killed.

I would spend the next year making drug runs for Billy. I worried constantly that I would get busted, or worse yet, that I would become the next body lying dead. I hated Billy with a passion, but fear kept me in line.

It was late 1965 when my luck turned around. My father opened a second dealership, in Oakland, and transferred Billy and a few others to the new location. I stayed at the San Francisco lot.

From that point forward I would only see Billy once a month, at employee meetings. I avoided Billy at all cost. Anytime he called the dealership and asked to speak with me, Katherine would tell him that I was either out or with a customer. Within time he just stopped calling.

Due to my fear and paranoia I changed my telephone number at home and about a month after Billy transferred, I moved.

I don't know why Billy let me get away so easily, but I believe he found someone else to do his dirty work for him.

For several years after that I would think of Billy everytime I heard of a body being found. I don't know how many people Billy shot to death, only one to my knowledge, but I wouldn't have been surprised to find out that he had gunned down a hundred. He was just that mean.

I never felt guilty about that guy being killed in front of me. The way I looked at the situation, it was between him and Billy, I was simply a by-stander. I never asked to be involved in any of that, and I'm thankful I got out when I did.

My life really took some wrong turns, but I eventually grew up and realized that every decision we make can be life altering.

12/16/06

My Dear Tina,

I hope today finds you well. Just a few days left before Christmas and I'm happy to report that I have finished my shopping and I am ready to see everyone.

I have many fond childhood memories of Christmas. It was always a major event for our family and it remained that way even after Diana and I married and began our own family.

During our marriage there was one Christmas that Diana and I did not spend together. It was not that we chose to be apart, but fate sometimes has a funny way of interrupting one's plans.

It was the week before Christmas, 1969, and I had went with some friends on a hunting trip to Texas. Not that I was a hunter, but these trips were more of a guys getaway. Two trips every year. One in the summer, one in the winter. Our winter trip usually took place between Thanksgiving and Christmas. Never so close to Christmas as this particular year, but due to other commitments, this was the only week that we could all get together. We would be back home 2 days before Christmas.

Diana had a keen understanding why these trips were so important, and never asked me not to go. She supported me completely and seemed to comprehend the importance of getting away and just "being a guy."

The 1969 trip was a 7 day adventure to Childress county in northern Texas. We chose this area for 2 reasons; the first being we had never been, the second being one of our buddies, Mark, had family there and we could stay at their ranch.

Again, keep in mind, I was not a hunter! None of us could be called hunters. We basically used 'hunting' or 'fishing' as an excuse to just get away. Our trips always consisted of leaving town, going somewhere we had never been, partying like we would never party again, and then returning home with great memories and plans for our next adventure.

However, Mark failed to tell us that his family was very much involved in hunting and had great plans for making this a trip of a lifetime!

There were five of us on this trip and we were thrilled to find that we had our own cabin on the property. Marks family owned over 1000 acres in quite possibly one of the most beautiful places I had ever been. On the property was the main house, where Marks uncle lived, and two smaller homes which were inhabited by Marks cousins and their families. There were also four cabins. The family typically rented the cabins out to tourists or the influx of hunters and fishermen during various times of the year.

Gorgeous streams ran throughout the property and there was a very large pond. The driveways leading up to the main house, as well as the two smaller homes, were tree lined, and the cabins were tucked quietly away.

As I stepped out of the car and took my first deep breath I could smell the intoxicating aroma of burning firewood. The smoke was gently floating through the air and could be seen escaping from the chimney of the main house.

The air was crisp and there was a light breeze. I placed my hands in my pockets and followed Mark to the cabin. Leaves were scattered along the walkway and I could hear them crunch as we walked on them.

The cabin was rustic and had Diana been with me I would have considered it cozy. There was a very large fireplace, an over sized couch, and two cushiony chairs. Cut wood was stacked on the floor next to the fireplace and the walls displayed photographs of white tail deer. The cabin had three bedrooms and a loft space.

Mark and I wandered around the cabin and since we were the first one's to arrive, we chose our rooms for the week.

Shortly after we finished our tour, we went outside and retrieved our belongings. Once back inside we made ourselves at home. While Mark got a fire going I stocked the refrigerator with beer and then lit up a joint. The other guys arrived nearly an hour after us, and we spent the rest of the evening drinking, smoking pot, and eating everything in sight.

It was 3am when we were rudely awaken by banging at the front door. As I made my way into the living room I found Mark standing there with his uncle and one of his cousins. It was time to hunt! What? Time to hunt? We just went to bed a couple hours earlier. The rest of the guys had now joined us in the living room and we were given 5 minutes to get dressed.

Tina, there's something wrong about leaving a warm bed to go out into the woods in the hopes that something may come walking past so that I might shoot it. It was freezing out there and I couldn't have shot anything had it walked up to me and posed.

We would spend the next 5 days out in those woods. Up every morning at 3am, back to the cabin every afternoon by 2 or 3pm, and then drink, eat and party until pure exhaustion drove us to bed.

On day six I woke up, got dressed, and as I made my way into the living room I was greeted by the other guys who all had huge smiles on their faces. No hunting for us today! There had been a blizzard the night before! A what? I walked to the door and there it was... more snow than I had ever seen in my life. The guys all headed back to their warm beds and I grabbed my jacket and walked outside.

The snow was beautiful. Just as I was about to walk off the porch I realized that I needed my camera. I went back inside, retrieved my camera, and journeyed out into the night.

The snow seemed to have a bluish tint. The moonlight was casting shadows and I was drawn to the trees; which oddly enough, seemed eerily seductive.

I would spend 2 hours capturing images of the snow, trees, footprints in the snow, and the most beautiful white tailed deer that one could only imagine. There they stood, posing for me! And, I shot them! It was in that moment that I thanked God that during our hunting trips I never saw the first deer. I was not responsible for eliminating one of these creatures for sport. The snow continued to fall during the course of the day, and we realized that we would not be heading home the next morning. As I walked to the main house I silently wondered how I was going to explain this to Diana, and how upset she was going to be when she realized that I would not be home for Christmas.

The phone rang five times before Diana answered. When I asked her what took so long for her to pick up the phone she told me that she was in the kitchen preparing my favorite Christmas goodies. I immediately felt as if the wind had been knocked out of me.

I explained to Diana that we were snowed in, and there was no way for us to get out of there. Diana said nothing. Dead silence. I stood there, imagining the look on her face, and without warning Diana simply said "I understand. It's okay. We'll just have Christmas when you do get home!"

Four days later I stepped through our front door and was greeted by Diana. She threw her arms around me and kissed me more passionately than ever before. I dropped my bags on the floor and as we continued to kiss we moved toward the couch.

Diana and I made love as if it were our first time together. I clearly remember wanting her so badly that it hurt. My body ached for her and as we made love we gazed into each others eyes.

Every move of Diana's body reminded me that she was the reason I was born. I believed then, and I still believe today, that I was born to love her.

I was lying on my back and Diana was on top of me. I couldn't take my eyes off of her. Her long hair was pulled back in a pony tail and she wore large, silver hoop earrings. Her face was void of makeup and her head was titled back. My eyes followed her neck down to her breasts and my hands ran up her body. First her thighs, then her hips; across her flat stomach and up to her breasts. I cupped her breasts with my hands and gently began to squeeze her nipples.

Diana's movements became quicker and I realized that I couldn't hold on any longer. Diana cried out and as she reached orgasm I erupted inside her. This was the first time that we reached orgasm at the exact same time. I had never experienced that before and was pleased that it was with Diana.

And to all a good night -

Love, C. J

Chapter 4
Life After Alcatraz

01/01/07

Happy New Year!

As I was preparing to write to you today I thought about New Years Day 1972. That was the day Diana and I moved into our first home. Up until then we had rented a house in the San Francisco Bay area.

January 1, 1972 was a very exciting time for us. Our son was a little over a year old and we had just purchased our first home. We had actually closed on the house a few days before Christmas, but decided to wait until the New Year to move in. It would have been too much to be moving during the Christmas holiday.

Jake and Sandra were there helping; mostly making sure that no one trampled on their "little man", and the rest of us were doing the physical work.

Once everything had been moved into the house we all decided to go grab a bite for dinner. Diana wanted to take a shower before heading to the restaurant, but encouraged me to go ahead without her; she would be along shortly. The restaurant was only a couple of blocks from the house, so we all left and Diana caught up about a half hour later.

When Diana entered the restaurant she looked absolutely stunning. She wore a knee length black skirt, a pink sweater, and black high heeled boots. Her hair was down and her make up was perfect She also wore a black wool coat that hit her at the hips.

Diana approached the table and I stood up, kissed her on the cheek and proceeded to pull out her chair. Diana smiled, but it was a smile that I couldn't recall ever having seen before. It was a coy smile; as if she knew something that I did not know.

81

During dinner that evening I caught Diana looking at me on several occasions. I wanted to take her by the hand, lead her somewhere private and ask her what she had on her mind, but I waited. If Diana had a secret I was going to let her tell me in her own time.

After dinner and much conversation we left the restaurant. Diana and I walked home, hand in hand, and when we reached our front door I scooped Diana up and carried her across the threshold. It may sound kind of silly, but I always wanted to do that.

Once inside I put Diana down and she grabbed me by the hand and led me into our bedroom. Now I knew what Diana's secret was! The room was filled with roses and burning candles.

I wondered how she was able to accomplish all of this in such a short period of time, but I would have to ask later.

Diana pushed me back onto the bed and began unbuttoning my shirt. Her hands slowly caressed my chest and then ran down to my waist. Diana unbuttoned and unzipped my jeans and then slowly pulled them off. As she moved back towards me I felt her tongue run across my thigh. With her hand firmly in place, she guided me into her mouth. She began slowly but within minutes her head was moving up and down in a quick, steady motion.

My eyes were closed and I was running my hands through Diana's hair. Diana must have sensed that I was on the verge of climaxing because she slowed down and began to stroke me with her hand. I felt her mouth kiss my stomach and then move up my chest. Her lips were now firmly on mine and I eased her onto her back. We continued to kiss and Diana continued to stroke me. My hand ran up her thigh and I pushed her skirt above her waist. I wanted to bring Diana to the same level of excitement that I was experiencing. As my fingers moved between Diana's legs I discovered that Diana had not been wearing anything under her skirt.

I pulled Diana's sweater off of her and lowered my head to her breasts. My hand ran back down her body and found it's place between her legs. As I pulled her nipple into my mouth I increased the intensity and speed of the strokes my hand was making. Diana, in turn, increased hers.

I absolutely couldn't wait any longer. I moved from my side and positioned myself in front of Diana. With my hands I spread her legs further apart and I pushed my way inside her with one quick thrust. My hands were firmly planted on her breasts and I couldn't take my eyes off her face.

Diana and I made love for nearly an hour. I remember this night vividly because afterwards, as we were lying in bed, Diana whispered "We have a new home, a happy and healthy little boy, and another one on the way."

My eyes flew open and Diana kissed me. We were expecting our second child! Now I knew Diana's secret. Eight months later we welcomed Isabella into our little family! Daddy's little girl.

Happy New Year my dear!

C.J.

01/07/07

Hello My Dear,

I was thinking about life after Alcatraz this week and I thought I would write you about that very subject.

It was a about a month after Diana and I had moved into our new home when I received a phone call at work. Diana was on the phone and speaking so quickly that I couldn't quite understand what she was telling me.

After determining that no one had died I was able to think clearly and listen to what she was saying.

Jake had telephoned Diana to tell her that Alcatraz had become part of the Golden Gate National Recreation Area.

Both Jake and Sandra were a bit surprised to hear this news and slightly upset about it. Alcatraz island had been their home and now it would appear that it was going to become a tourist attraction. Diana had also felt the sting upon hearing this news.

Diana had grown up on Alcatraz island; it was literally the only home she had ever known. It was difficult to see her family leave the island, but this was the end of an era.

Diana was talking so fast and she was noticeably upset. I hung up the phone with her and walked into my fathers office. I explained the situation, and went home.

When I arrived at the house I found Diana sitting at the kitchen table crying. I tried to comfort her, but I didn't really comprehend how she was feeling.

Diana calmed down enough to tell me that she would never be able to look across the bay again and see Alcatraz the same way she had always seen it. Now it was just going to be another tourist attraction. Visitors toAlcatraz would see it as a famous prison; not as her home. No one would appreciate the fact that Alcatraz was much more than that. Alcatraz, although it had a reputation as being "The Rock", "Escape Proof" and the home to some of the nations most infamous inmates, it was so much more than that.

Dianas memories of Alcatraz were of a life filled with joy and love. Playing on the island and growing up to care and appreciate the beauty of what was Alcatraz.

Diana and I had fallen in love on that island. We were married on that island. On several occasions we had been trapped on that island, but never complained about it. How do you complain about being trapped in paradise? And for us, Alcatraz had been paradise.

As I listened to Diana my own memories came flooding back. Alcatraz had only been a part of my life for four and a half years, but it had been the backdrop to so many important events in my life.

Diana and I sat there at that kitchen table for hours. We reminisced over our life there together, and then we headed over to the pier.

Once there we found a bench and just stared out at Alcatraz Island. We were there to say goodbye to Alcatraz. We were saying goodbye to an old friend.

As we stood up to leave I kissed Diana on the forehead and then whispered in her ear "Alcatraz will never be what it once was, but we experienced a piece of history. Perhaps no one else will ever know what that island meant to us, but we will never forget."

Alcatraz officially opened for tourists in 1972.

01/22/07

Hello my Friend!

I have been quite busy recently trying to organize my home office. Diana has been on me for as far back as I can remember about the constant mess and clutter, so I finally decided to do something about it. I imagined days filled with complete and utter boredom, but as I sifted through old papers and photographs I came across something I thought you might find interesting, so I scanned them and I'm including as an attachment in this e-mail.

What you are looking at are index cards that Alcatraz kept on inmates and yes, one is of Al Capone and the other is of Theodore Cole.

At this point you may be wondering how and why I have these. Truth be known, I had actually forgotten that they were in my possession. But as I sifted through a box labeled 1971 I found them!

You have probably figured out by now that I haven't always been an upstanding, fine young man. Tina, I actually stole these cards the day Jake and Sandra left Alcatraz Island. We had just finished loading their belongings onto the barge and Jake went back to the house to make sure that nothing had been left behind. I decided to go inside the prison for one last look around. As I was taking mental notes and snapping a few photographs I heard Jake calling for me. For reasons still unknown to me, I reached my hand into a small box and grabbed. I shoved what I had into my Jacket pocket and it wasn't until I was back at home that night did I pull the cards out and discover that I had Capone's and Cole's.

I never told Diana that I had taken the index cards; I simply threw them in a file folder and forgot about them.

I have no idea if anyone ever missed them and I certainly have no idea if they're worth anything, but perhaps I will leave them to my children after I'm gone. Who knows, maybe I'll include a letter with them explaining how they came to be in my possession.

I often wonder about something... if you never tell your children about your life and who you were, what you did, and how you came to be the person you became, do they really know you? Or, do they simply know the person you allowed them to know?

The older I become the more I realize that I don't want to die someday and people only know the person I allowed them to know. I want my family and friends to remember me as I truly was. Faults and all! That's who I am. I am an imperfect soul that has known right from wrong, but lived my life at times as if I didn't. I do believe that I'm a good person deep down inside, but it would seem that I have had a tendency to push things to the edge a little more frequently than most.

At the end of the day though, this is who I am. I have come to the conclusion that it's the events of my life that have made me the man I am today. Perhaps I have not always done the right thing, but I have learned from my mistakes, and this is the man that I want my children and grandchildren to remember.

I will definitely leave these index cards to my children and I will include a letter on how they came to be in my possession. Now that I think about it, I am going to begin writing several letters. If my story will ever be told to my children I want it to be told by me. After all, if not with my own words, then how could the story ever be correct?

Thank you Tina!

You're always there to listen and you allow me to ramble on about my life. I often wonder what you think about this crazy old man, but then for some reason, I get the feeling that you "get me."

Love C. J

02/13/07

Good Morning!

I am writing to you very early today, 4 am to be exact. I had a very restless night and as I lay in bed contemplating watching television or continuing my struggle for sleep I found myself thinking of another restless night some thirty plus years ago.

Diana and the children had gone with Jake and Sandra to Seattle to visit Diana's older sister for a few days; she had recently endured a divorce and had just settled into a new home. It had been quite a while since I had been left home alone and it being the weekend I found time passing very slowly.

The first day was quite enjoyable; it was a friday and I left work early. I picked up some beer on my way home and once I arrived I popped the top and watched a bit of television. The fun really began as my friends arrived for an all night poker game.

The next morning I slept in and after a quick shower I debated on how I should spend the rest of the day. A long walk? Grab a bite to eat? Maybe a movie? I hadn't quite made up my mind, but I knew I wasn't going to just sit at home.

I threw on a pair of jeans and an old sweatshirt and headed over to a local restaurant for a burger. It was fairly cool outside but I enjoyed the walk and instead of going straight to the restaurant I made my way to the pier.

I stood there and watched a large number of people board the ferry that was headed to Alcatraz. As they boarded I caught a glimpse of a beautiful blonde woman that somehow had a look of familiarity. I wondered if I knew her from somewhere, but quickly surmised that I couldn't possibly, because there was no way I could ever forget a woman that beautiful. I continued to watch the ferry as it left the dock and made it's way to Alcatraz Island.

Hunger had began to set in and I decided to go grab that burger. As I entered the little burger joint I quickly spotted an old neighbor, who waved at me to come join him. I placed my order, paid for it, and the cashier handed me my tray of greasy goodness. As I approached the booth that Johnny was sitting at he extended his arm and we shook hands.

As I scarfed down my burger and fries I explained to him that Diana and the children were in Seattle for a few days and he explained to me that his wife was gone too, but permanently! She had filed for a divorce. He said it as if he didn't care, but his eyes told a different story. I immediately felt bad for him and I couldn't keep myself from wondering how I would be able to deal with losing Diana. I knew that losing Diana would never be an option.

Johnny continued to discuss his pending divorce and then suggested we go shoot some pool and have a few drinks. It was still rather early in the day and I certainly was not dressed to go out; at least no where respectable. I found myself looking for excuses not to go, but Johnny looked as if he really could use a friend, so I agreed to meet with him later that evening.

As 7pm approached I once again began looking for some excuse not to go, but again began feeling guilty, so I headed over to the club.

As I entered the nightclub the music was so loud I could barely hear myself think. The place was jam packed and the dance floor was so crowded that it didn't seem as if one *more person would fit. It had been quite a while since I had been to a club, at least without Diana, and I couldn't help but notice all the beautiful women. I seemed to be noticing everything about them. Their hair, their smiles, their bodies. I actually caught myself laughing! Two days without Diana and my mind was going places it hadn't been in quite a long time! I made my way to the bar, ordered a rum and coke and headed over to the pool tables. I immediately spotted Johnny, who was already playing a game with an older gentleman. We shook hands and I found a bar stool up against the wall, sat down and waited for their game to be over.*

Johnny and I shot pool for a couple of hours and I managed to drink a couple more rum and cokes. I was feeling pretty good and having a much better time than I anticipated. Johnny headed over to the mens room and as I began to rack the balls it happened. I felt a tap on my shoulder and as I turned around I instantly recognized the person standing in front of me. It was the beautiful blonde from the pier.

She said hello and then told me that she noticed my partner had left and asked if she could play a game with me. I told her that he only went to the mens room, but I was sure he wouldn't mind if she took his place for a little while.

I finished racking and I let her break. I never noticed when Johnny came back because this woman was absolutely captivating. She was very likeable and I found myself completely and utterly drawn to her.

I won that game and Christie offered to buy me a drink. Her name was Christie. Johnny jumped back up and was ready to play so Christie ordered us each a drink and we spent the next couple of hours shooting pool, laughing and drinking.

As midnight approached Johnny said goodnight and left me and Christie on our own. For one brief moment I began to think logically and told Christie that I enjoyed meeting her and it was a lot of fun, but I needed to get going as well. Christie agreed and asked me if I would mind walking her out.

As we left the club I asked her if she lived nearby and that's when she told me that she didn't live in San Francisco at all. She was here on business and was staying at the Holiday Inn, which was 4 blocks from the club. She seemed a bit tipsy so I offered to walk her to the hotel.

God as my witness, I never intended to do anything else with Christie, but as we approached the hotel Christie asked me if I wanted to go up to her room and I said yes.

As I sit here today, thinking back on that night, I could easily tell you that I was drunk. I made a mistake. I temporarily lost my mind. But, I would be lying. The truth of the matter is this: Men have a desire to conquer. We need to know that women, other than our wives, find us attractive. Regardless of how much we love our wives, we have a need for excitement. We have this built in mechanism that says 'Yeah, go for it!" We get bored with our wives and we get bored with ourselves.

Tina, I wish I could say that during my marriage I was one of the few men out there that never cheated. In my heart I was always faithful, and I know you've heard this before, but there is a difference between love and sex. Men seem more capable of distinguishing between the two. If I have sex with someone other than my wife it doesn't mean I no longer love my wife, and it most certainly doesn't mean that I love the other woman. It's just sex.

As I left that hotel room the next morning I tried to convince myself of that, but it wasn't working. I felt immense regret for my actions and I wished I could turn back time.

You may be wondering if I told Diana of my indiscretion. I did not. There would be nothing to be gained and if I told her I would only be hurting her. Why would I do that? To make my self feel better? To release the guilt that I was feeling?

Diana came home on monday, and later that night, after we made love, I endured a very restless night. As I watched my wife sleeping I kept reminding myself that it was only sex.

02/27/07

Dear Tina,

Hope today finds you well. I visited the cemetery today where Jake and Sandra are buried and it occurred to me that I have not shared with you their passing.

The date was February 27, 1979. Jake and Sandra had spent the morning shopping followed by a long lunch at one of their favorite cafe's. After returning home Jake received a phone call from his brother, who lived in Oakland at the time, inviting him and Sandra to dinner.

They arrived at Lou and Marcie's house around 6pm and the four enjoyed the evening. Marcie had prepared a pot roast, which every member of the family knows is the only thing she could prepare well, and they spent several hours sitting at the table and reminiscing.

It was 10pm when Jake and Sandra headed home. At exactly 10:27pm a car that was traveling at speeds more than 90 mph struck their vehicle. Sandra was killed instantly and within minutes of arriving at the hospital Jake was pronounced dead.

I will always remember receiving that phone call. Diana was soaking in the bath tub and I had just checked in on the kids. I was walking towards our bedroom when the phone rang.

As I placed the phone back on the receiver I realized that I would have to tell Diana that her mother was dead and her father was being transported to the hospital. I felt the tears swelling up in my eyes and before I could stop them they were rolling down my face.

With every fiber of my being I wanted to just sit there and let Diana enjoy her bath. I knew that the moment I told her our lives would never be the same. Our children's lives would never be the same. I wanted time to stand still, at least for a few more minutes.

As I entered the bathroom Diana was drying off. She looked up at me and asked me what was wrong. I walked over to her and I wrapped my arms around her waist. I gently kissed her on the forehead and told her that there had been an accident and we needed to get to the hospital. Diana asked me who was in the accident and I told her that it was Jake and Sandra.

She must have known it was bad. The look on my face must have told her it was really bad because the tears started falling. I took Diana by the hand and led her to our bed. She sat down on the edge of the bed and I kneeled on the floor in front of her. Diana was crying, I was crying and as her hands ran through my hair I told her that her mother had been killed.

As Diana dressed I reached for the phone and called our next door neighbor. The children were asleep and I couldn't bear the thought of waking them to change their lives forever. They could wait for this news. Our neighbor came over and stayed at the house and Diana and I left for the hospital.

Diana cried the entire way and there were moments when I had difficulty seeing the road through my own tears.

As we made our way across the parking lot, into the hospital and to the desk, Diana's grip on my hand became tighter. We told the nurse at the desk who we were and she pointed down the hall and told us to wait in the second room. The doctor would be right with us.

Moments later a young man wearing scrubs entered the room. He asked us if we were Jake's children and we said yes. He then said "I'm sorry, but your father died shortly after arrival. There was nothing we could do. His internal injuries were fatal."

I don't remember much after that. Diana fell to her knees and I wrapped my arms around her. I wanted to take her pain away. I wanted to take my pain away. I wanted to say "It's gonna be okay", but I knew that would be a lie.

I vaguely remember the drive back home. I vaguely remember the days that followed that fateful night. I do, however, remember the moment that Diana and I told our children that Nana and Papa were gone. Diana tried, but couldn't hold the tears at bay. The children were so young and I vividly remember thinking how they were cheated. Diana and I both worried that in time they would forget their grandparents. It was shortly after the funeral when Diana and I decided that we would continue to celebrate Jake and Sandra's birthdays. We also vowed that every year, on the date of the accident, that we would all visit them at the cemetery. Our children would never forget Jake and Sandra. We would never let them.

Today we remember

C.J.

Chapter 5
A New Day

03/09/07

Dear Tina,

As I continue to weed through the disaster that is my home office I continue to find items from my past that reminds me of just how lucky I am and what a remarkable life I have lived.

The love that Diana and I have shared is truly nothing short of a miracle. I have spent every day of my life, since the age of 23, being grateful. Finding little treasures that I had long forgotten about makes me even more grateful.

I realize that as we communicate between each other you only read my words. Today I am going to share with you Diana's words. This was a note I received one day out of the blue, for no particular reason:

My dear sweet husband,

I wanted to let you know that even after 15 years of marriage I still look at you and thank God that you're mine.

We are so lucky to have each other and to be able to raise our children in a loving home. This morning while you were still asleep I stood at the bedroom door and wondered what my life would have been had I not met you.

I love you so much! I cannot remember life before you and I cannot imagine life without you

Thank you for being the husband that I didn't even have the capability of dreaming about.

I only hope that I continue to be the wife that you fell in love with. I like to think that somehow, in small way, I have made you as happy as you have made me.

With all my love,

Diana

Tina, after all these years this little note still brings tears to me eyes. I only wish everyone could know the love that I have for my wife.

Talk soon

C.J.

"Hello?"

"Good Morning Sunshine!"

"C. J. Good Morning! How are you today?"

"I'm wonderful! I hope I didn't wake you"

I looked over at the clock and realized that it was already 8am. C. J. had not waken me, but I was rather surprised how quickly the morning was flying by. I had been awake since 5am and had already spent three hours reading C. J.'s e-mail messages.

"No, you did not wake me. I've actually been up for a while now. I guess my body is still on central time!"

C. J. let out a laugh and then proceeded to tell me that he already had the day planned.

"I was thinking that I could meet you at the hotel and perhaps we could go for a walk. Then of course lunch and if you're up to it I thought we may take a drive! I would love to show you around the old neighborhood!"

C. J. sounded exuberant and I was up for anything. I felt like a teenage girl about to meet her idol!

"That sounds great C. J. What time should I expect you?"

"I should be there right about 10, if that's good with you?"

"I'll be ready!"

"Fine then! I'll meet you in the lobby at 10 and we'll just see where the day takes us!"

As I hung the phone up I felt a bit nervous. I gathered C. J.'s e-mail messages and placed them back in the file folder. My fingers shuffled through all of C. J.'s messages until I found the photo's. There was C. J. and Diana on their wedding day at Alcatraz. *Where's the other picture?* I suddenly became panicked.

Where's the picture of C. J.??? I sat down on the edge of the bed and began removing each letter from the file folder and then I found it. The last photo that C. J. had sent me.

As I held that photograph in my hand I studied it like I had never studied it before. *Forty years later and he hasn't really changed! Oh, of course there's the obvious changes, more salt in his hair than pepper, a few more laugh lines around his eyes, but other than that C. J. looked pretty much the same as he did forty years ago.*

I glanced back at the wedding picture and then back at the more recent picture and for the first time I admitted to myself that C. J. was an extremely good looking man. I began to wonder if his story would have been so interesting if he had not been as attractive as he is.

I imagined him in his early twenties and wondered how and why he got into the things that he got into. I also realized that it was no surprise that he never seemed to have a shortage of women wanting and willing to go to bed with him. After all, he had managed to hook Diana, who was every bit as beautiful as he was handsome; perhaps even more so!

It suddenly occurred to me that C. J. was a bad boy. The kind of man that certain women are drawn to. A bit mysterious, a bit dangerous, and all the while coming across as innocent. I could understand how any woman could look into his eyes and believe anything that he said. C. J. had that quality about him. I found myself looking at those photographs and smiling. *Yep... C. J. could charm the pants off anyone I bet!*

I placed C. J.'s e-mail messages back into the file folder, along with the photo's, and then walked over to the in room safe. After setting a new code for the safe and tucking the folder away I walked into the rest room and started my shower. It was time to meet C. J.

As I entered the elevator I felt light headed and for a moment I thought I may throw up. It was 9:50 and I wondered if C. J. was already in the lobby. *I hope not! I hope I get there first and*

101

can calm my ass down! Why the hell am I so nervous anyway?* I
kept telling myself that it's only C. J., not a famous celebrity or
something. *Jesus Christ...get a grip!*

As I exited the elevator my eyes darted across the lobby. *Thank
you God! He's not here yet!* I made my way over to a chair near the
fireplace and sat down. *I need a cigarette! I wonder if I have time
to go outside and smoke one?* I reached for my purse and jumped
up.

"You're not leaving already are you?"

I quickly turned around and there he was. I couldn't get any
words out. I stood there in complete awe. C. J. walked directly
toward me and before I knew it he wrapped his arms around me
and kissed me on my cheek.

"Are you okay?" C. J. asked and I could see a look of concern
on his face.

I somehow found the ability to smile and reassured C. J.
that I was fine. "You startled me! I realized that I was about ten
minutes early and was going to step outside and smoke a cigarette!
I didn't expect you to come walking up behind me!"

C. J. laughed and explained that he had arrived a few minutes
earlier than planned so he had made a dash into the rest room.
"Gotta make sure I look good! Well, at least as good as one can
look at this age!" I found myself still smiling and now laughing.

As C. J. began to tell me how unusually light traffic was this
morning I just kept looking at him. *What is he? 5'10" maybe?
No... probably 5'11". Damn... look at those brown eyes! Good
at that age? He looks good for any age!* C. J. continued to tell me
about some crazy taxi driver and I continued to take inventory.
I wanted to be "in the moment" with C. J., but was finding it
difficult to concentrate.

I noticed that every hair on C. J.'s head was perfectly messed
up. Not in a sloppy type of way, but in a sexy type of way. His
hair is curly and it reminded me of my own on lazy days. Wash
it, scrunch it with your hands, and you're done. I also noticed
that he had not shaved. He had a 5 O'clock shadow at 10 O'clock

in the morning. My eyes continued to study his face, all the while smiling and nodding my head as C. J. chatted. *Mmmmm... perfect teeth!* He had a movie star smile and my eyes continued to size C. J. up.

Baby blue oxford shirt with white pinstripes, sleeves rolled up to just below his elbows. Faded blue jeans and dark brown, well worn, boat shoes. C. J.'s shirt wasn't tucked in and as he stood there in front of me I realized that in person he reminded me of someone, but who? *Why can't I put my finger on it???*

"So, you ready to go for a walk? We couldn't have asked for better weather!"

"Huh? Oh! Yes! I'm ready!" *Oh, My, God! He's going to think I'm an idiot! Get it together!*

C. J. and I walked out of the hotel and he pointed toward Alcatraz. "I can't believe that I'm actually going back there tomorrow."

I looked up at C. J. and saw what I thought to be sadness. For a brief second I wasn't sure what I should say. Just as I was about to open my mouth C. J. jumped in and saved me.

"It's not that I have bad feelings about Alcatraz. Just the contrary really. Alcatraz is like an old friend that I haven't seen in a while. I vowed I would never go back and now that I am going back I guess I'm feeling conflicted. Alcatraz is a different place than it was all those years ago."

I smiled at C. J. and then asked him what I really wanted to know, "Why then are we going?"

C. J. stopped dead in his tracks and I turned to face him.

"Well, we're going back because Diana wants to go back. If it were up to me my last memories would be of the day we moved Jake and Sandra out of there. The things we do for the one's we love, huh?"

I smiled slightly and replied with the first thought that came to mind, 'You know C. J., you and Diana live here, you could go to Alcatraz anytime you want. Why tomorrow and why did you want me to be here?"

C. J. smiled at me and without hesitation he answered. "Well, like I said, I never planned on going back to Alcatraz. This is all Diana's idea. I wanted you to be here because I've shared so many stories and memories of Alcatraz with you. I thought it would only be right if you were with us when we go back. You may not understand that right now, but before this trip is over you will. Please bear with me. I promise, you will understand."

C. J. most definitely could lay on the charm.

Fine. He asked me to come, I'm here. Certainly I can wait one more day to find out why.

C. J. and I continued our walk and our small talk. There wasn't a subject we didn't cover. Kids, grandkid's, photography, life in the south, life in the west and love and marriage.

It was nearly 2 pm when we decided we were hungry and it was time to eat. C. J. recommended an Italian restaurant not too far from where we were standing, so that's where we headed.

We entered the restaurant and shortly after we were seated a gentleman came to the table and shook C. J.'s hand.

"Bobby, this is a dear friend of mine who's visiting from Alabama. Tina, this is Bobby! Bobby owns this fine establishment!"

Bobby extended his arm and we shook hands. After a moment of chit chat Bobby declared that he was going to send out a bottle of his finest wine. I secretly wondered if C. J. hadn't planned all of this, but I gushed over how sweet that was of him.

"I have known Bobby for what seems like forever" C. J. announced.

"I got the impression that the two of you knew each other fairly well!"

C. J. smiled and then leaned in toward me, "You know, this place is really special."

I returned the smile and with a fair amount of sarcasm I looked C. J. in the eyes, "Oh? Why is that? Do they have a special sauce?"

C. J. laughed. "Well, their sauce is very good! I don't know how special it is, but it's definitely good! I was actually referring to something else."

No way! There is no way! "C. J., are you going to tell me that this is the same Italian restaurant where you and Diana had your first date?"

C. J.'s smile went from ear to ear. "Yes! You remember! There have been some obvious changes over the years, but this is the place!"

Our server arrived with the wine and a basket of bread and proceeded to take our lunch order. C. J. and I spent the next two hours drinking wine, eating and continuing our small talk. Before I knew it my nervousness was gone and I felt as if I were spending the day with a long lost friend.

We left the restaurant and headed back to the hotel. Once there C. J. had valet retrieve his car and we headed out to see more of the city.

C. J. and I made our way along the streets of San Francisco and I found myself hanging on to his every word. He pointed out where his fathers car lot was, where he and Diana's first home was, and the cemetery where Jake and Sandra were buried. Then he pulled the car over in front of a huge Victorian style house. Before I knew it C. J. had put the car in park and stepped outside. I immediately followed.

"Where are we?" I asked.

C. J. walked over to the house and sat down on the steps. I stood in front of him. "What are we doing here C. J.?"

"See that bay window? On the second floor?"

C. J. didn't have to say anything else. I knew exactly where we were. *Sam!* I sat down on the step next to C. J. and placed my hand on his back.

"Are you okay?" I asked.

"You know, I've done a lot of things that I'm not proud of, and most I have learned to live with, but I have never gotten over that girl falling out that window. If I could go back to that day I would have either stayed home or went with Diana to the Human-Be-In."

C. J. obviously had deep regret for what happened all those years ago and I felt bad for him. I couldn't help but feel that he had somehow been torturing himself all these years.

"C. J., you didn't mean for that to happen. It was an accident. You did the right thing, you went to the police. Don't you think it's time for you to forgive yourself?"

C. J. looked at me and I thought he would say something, but he never did. We just sat there. I wondered how often he comes here. I wondered how he managed to never tell Diana what had happened, and I wondered how Diana would react if she did know.

I didn't check my watch, but we had been sitting on those steps for quite a while. Suddenly C. J. seemed to get a burst of energy and he stood up, extended his hand to me, and we walked back to the car.

Once we were back on the road C. J. suggested that we head over to Golden Gate Park. I agreed and not much else was said. C. J. drove and I took in the sights.

We arrived at the park and I grabbed my camera from my bag. The sun was beginning to set and I wanted to capture the light as it hit the Golden Gate Bridge. C. J. just laughed. "Once a photographer always a photographer, huh?"

I laughed and then warned C. J. that he better be nice or I may start aiming my camera his way! Then, without warning, I did just that. As C. J. made his way toward the waters edge I stayed behind. Once he realized that I wasn't next to him or at least directly behind him, he turned around to find me and I started shooting.

"Hey! If I had known this was going to end up being a photo shoot I would have dressed better!"

"No you wouldn't have! And I wouldn't have wanted you to be anything but yourself!" I shot fifteen frames and made my way to C. J.

"This place is so beautiful. Especially this time of the day. I'm always amazed. It doesn't matter how many times I shoot this place the pictures are always different! And, as many photo's as I've seen, I have never seen two alike."

C. J. seemed to ponder my remarks momentarily and then replied, "Well, I guess that's because it would virtually be impossible to stand in the exact location, at the exact time of the day, using the exact camera with the exact settings. No two people are alike. No two photographers are alike. No two photo's are alike. Don't ya think?" I laughed and agreed. I wasn't expecting such reasoning over my comment, but there it was!

C. J. grabbed my hand and we began walking. Within minutes we approached the area directly under the bridge and C. J. sat down on a large boulder.

"This is one of my favorite places in San Francisco. Sometimes it's so packed with people that one can waste an entire day just people watching! Other times, like now, it's just a quiet place to reflect. I spend a lot of time here."

"Hmmmm... I think I can understand that. I wonder though, have you always been a person that likes to people watch or spend quiet time reflecting? Or, does that happen over time?"

C. J. seemed to be sifting through his thoughts. I thought he may be choosing his words carefully, unlike me. I have a tendency to say whatever comes to mind without really thinking about it first.

"Ya know Tina, I think it happens over time. I think when we're young we just live our lives day to day. Then, as we become older, we seem more inclined to think things over and make sense of our lives."

"If you had to sum up your life in one word, what would that word be?"

C. J. stood up, walked over to me, and kissed me on the forehead, "You're gonna have to let me think about that for a few minutes!"

I, as usual, didn't give much thought to my response, "Take your time!"

The sky began to grow darker and C. J. put his arm around me. "You ready to head out?" he asked, his voice softer than it had been.

"Yep! Where we going now?"

"Well, let's head back toward the wharf. Maybe have a drink?"

I looked at C. J. and felt like there was something that I was missing. I'm pretty good at reading people, but C. J. was still a mystery that I couldn't quite put my finger on. "Let's go!" I replied.

We drove back to the hotel and let valet take the car. I glanced inside the hotel and noticed that the lobby was pretty quiet.

"Hey, you wanna grab a drink at the bar?"

C. J.'s eye's darted inside and he replied with a simple "Why not?"

C. J. and I walked through the lobby and over to the bar. I ordered a screwdriver and C. J. chose a rum and coke. After receiving our drinks we made our way over to the lounge area and settled into two club chairs sitting near the fireplace.

"Blessed" C. J. said.

"What?" I looked at C. J. trying to figure out what he was talking about.

"One word to sum up my life! Blessed!" C. J. smiled with a look of satisfaction.

"Oh! I didn't have a clue what you were talking about! Blessed, huh? You feel that you've had a blessed life?"

"I know I have! I'm still here, despite a million reasons for me not to be! I've received love and I've given love. I've raised two amazing children. My life has been blessed."

C. J. raised his glass to his lips and I studied him. I knew things about this man that I probably shouldn't know. I knew things about him that his wife of more than forty years didn't know. *What has brought me here?*

"You seem deep in thought," C. J. said in a near whisper.

"Oh, I'm sorry. No, not really. I was just thinking about the day. I really enjoyed seeing all the places that you've written about."

C. J. smiled and leaned forward. "I want you to know that I am thrilled that you're here. It seems so surreal. Before today I only knew *of* you, and I felt a certain freedom. I felt a level of familiarity with you and at the same time I knew that you didn't have any expectations of me. I think that's why I was able to tell you my inner most secrets. You were safe."

I didn't quite know how to reply to that and for the first time in my life I didn't just open my mouth and let the words come out. I took in what C. J. was saying and I understood the importance of it.

C. J. leaned back in his chair and closed his eyes. I took a sip of my drink and my mind began to wander. I found this man incredibly sexy, and if it were not for the fact that we're both married, I could easily imagine his hands on my body and the warmth of his breath on my face.

"Penny for your thoughts," C. J. was grinning.

"Oh, believe me, you don't want to know. I'm afraid they may embarrass you!"

C. J. laughed and came back with "Oh?! Do tell!"

I placed my drink on the table and leaned in closer to C. J. "I was just wondering...no, never mind!"

C. J.'s eye's opened wide and he reminded me of a kid at Christmas. I couldn't help but to laugh.

"Now wait a minute... I have told you more things about myself than I have ever told anyone! You know me better than anyone else on the planet! And you won't tell me what you were thinking?" C. J.'s voice was soft and he ran his hand through his hair.

"Okay... if you really want to know... I was wondering if you still feel safe with me? You said that you felt safe with me because we hadn't met and I had no expectations. Well, now I'm here. Do you still feel safe?"

Once again C. J. chose his words carefully. "I do feel safe. I still feel as if I can tell you anything. That's why I'm going to tell you this: You're lying! That's not what you were thinking. I can read you like a book and right now you're trying to figure out how to change the subject."

"Well done C. J.! You're right. That's not what I was thinking. I was thinking what might happen if neither one of us were married. I was thinking that you are perhaps the sexiest man I have ever met. Feel better now?"

C. J. leaned back in his chair and with a smile on his face he said "Yes, I do feel better!"

We finished our drinks and after making plans to meet at the pier the next morning we both stood up. C. J. placed his hand in mine and kissed me on the cheek.

"I had a wonderful day and I'm so glad you're here!"

I smiled at C. J. and said goodnight. As I turned toward the elevator I heard C. J. call out my name. I turned back to see him and he placed his hand on his heart. With a smile on his face he walked out the door.

As I entered my room I noticed the clock. It was 11:30 pm and I was pleased with the course the day had taken. I had been so nervous this morning and before the day was over I felt comfortable enough with C. J. to tell him that he was perhaps the sexiest man that I had ever met. *Oh My God! Did I really say that? Damn, blame it on the liquor!*

I kicked off my shoes and walked toward the rest room. I turned the water on, adjusted the temperature and began to fill the bath tub. I took two steps toward the vanity when I heard knocking on my door. *What the hell?*

"Who's there?" I asked.

"It's me, C. J. I need to talk to you."

I opened the door and there stood C. J. "What's wrong? We just spent the entire day talking. Did you forget something?"

C. J. grabbed my hands and I immediately thought about Tony Richter, the cop on the airplane.

"What is it C.J.?"

"I'm sorry Tina. I need to tell you something, and I have to tell you now! Can we go for a walk?"

My mind was racing and my heart was pounding. What does Oprah always say? *Never let them take you to a second location!* I didn't know what to do and then I realized that if he wanted to kill me he had the entire day to do it.

"C. J., I was just about to take a bath. The waters running."

C. J. looked at me as if he were in pain and then he said something that I will never forget.

"Tina, I'm so very sorry, but this can't wait. I need to tell you something and I need to tell you now. I've tried to find a way to tell you this all day, but the words just wouldn't come. Please, go for a walk with me. Just trust me."

In that moment I realized that I had no choice but to trust C. J. He had trusted me with his life. He had been open and honest and never held back. If C. J. needed to tell me something I needed to hear what it was.

"Okay. Let me put on my shoes and turn the water off."

C. J. and I left the hotel and walked toward Pier 39. Once there we found a bench and sat down. C. J. took my hands in his and tears began to run down his face. I remained silent, deciding that whatever C. J. had to say he would have to say it in his own time.

"Alcatraz...I realized I was in love with Diana and that realization came to me one night at Alcatraz. I fell in love with her there, I married her there, and tomorrow I will leave her there."

My head was spinning and I couldn't comprehend what C. J. was saying. His tears were flowing and I began to shake. *What does that mean? He'll leave her there?*

"C. J., I don't understand. I'm trying, but I just don't understand what you're saying."

C. J. wiped his tears, took a deep breath and ran his hands through his hair. He suddenly appeared much older than he had throughout the day.

"I wanted to tell you this earlier. Not just earlier today, but earlier. Last year. I wanted to write you and tell you, but I just couldn't bring myself to do it. I think I was in denial. Perhaps shock. If the words came out of my mouth, or if I wrote them down, then that would make them true. One year ago tomorrow, well, today now, one year ago today Diana passed away."

What? I felt ill. My head started to pound and my stomach was queasy. I wanted to throw up. Without warning tears ran down my face. I could hardly see C. J. and I was now shaking uncontrollably. I was trying to get myself together and make sense of what he was saying, but I couldn't. I started to read his letters in my mind. *Hadn't he referred to Diana in the past year? What did he write when he asked me to come out here?* I wanted to scream. I wanted answers.

I wiped the tears away and grabbed C. J.'s hand. He needed to tell me and I needed to hear him.

"It was so unexpected Tina. I don't even know where to begin. So much of that day is a blur to me. I had left the house that morning around 7 am... nothing important to do, but it was a beautiful morning, a lot like today, and I decided to go for a walk. Diana was still in bed, but she woke up as I was walking out of the bedroom. She raised up and asked me where I was going. I walked over to her, kissed her, and told her that I was going for a walk. I asked her if she needed anything while I was out and she said no. I left the house and returned about an hour later. I was surprised that Diana wasn't in the kitchen or sitting at the breakfast bar enjoying her first cup of coffee, but I had only been gone for an hour so I assumed she was taking a shower. I started the coffee maker and walked into the bedroom. The shower wasn't running."

C. J. paused for a moment, but this time I didn't think he was choosing his words. This time it seemed that he was searching for words. He visually appeared stressed and I wanted to just turn back time. I didn't want to know the details and I wanted to go back to not knowing. I wanted the love affair between C.J. and Diana to continue.

"I looked over at the bed and wondered why she was still there. Diana has never been a late sleeper and once awake she stays awake. I don't know how I knew it, but I knew something was wrong. I called out her name, but there was no reply. I sat down on the edge of the bed and held her hand, which was warm. I then lowered my head to her face and realized she was still breathing. I grabbed for the telephone on the night stand and dialed 911. I remember telling the 911 operator that yes, she's breathing. No, she's not conscious. I was frantic and time seemed to stand still."

I couldn't stop the tears from flowing as I listened to C. J. recount the last moments of Diana's life. I continued to hold his hand and listened as carefully as I could.

"It seemed like forever, but the ambulance finally arrived. I wanted to go with her, but they kept telling me there was no room. I would have to meet them there. My next door neighbor had came out as they were putting Diana in the ambulance and he drove me to the hospital. I cried the entire way and found myself praying for the first time in years."

C.J. stopped talking and stood up. I was still holding onto his hand and he never let go. I stood up and we began to walk closer to the dock. We were looking out across the bay and C.J. never broke his gaze from Alcatraz.

"When we arrived at the hospital my neighbor let me out at the emergency room entrance and he went to park the car. I rushed inside and to the desk. I kept saying her name... Diana... where's Diana? A nurse came out and told me that they were doing everything they could do to help Diana and they would let me know what was going on as soon as they knew something. I needed to take a seat and wait. Jim, my neighbor, sat down beside me and neither one of us said a word. I felt like a condemned man waiting for his execution. I wanted someone to tell me what was going on, but at the same time fearing what they would say."

C.J. stopped there, gathering his thoughts.

"This is where my recollection of events goes foggy. I remember a Doctor. I remember walking into a small, private room. I remember hearing *I'm sorry* and I remember hearing *massive heart attack.* I still try to understand that. Diana did everything right. She ate right, she exercised, she never smoked, and she rarely drank. How could this be happening? I remember falling to my knees and someone's arm around me. Then I remember being told that I could see Diana.

"I walked back into the emergency room and a nurse pointed behind a curtain. I was shaking and crying and I felt fear unlike anything I had ever felt before. I walked over to Diana and I held her hand. She looked so peaceful...so beautiful. I leaned over, kissed her on the forehead and told her how sorry I was. I was sorry I had left her that morning. I was sorry it was her lying there and not me. I was sorry that I didn't tell her I loved her before I went for my morning walk. *Why didn't I tell her I loved her?* A day has never passed that I didn't tell Diana I loved her. Why that day?"

I wanted to tell C. J. that it was okay, that Diana knew he loved her, but I couldn't get the words out. C. J. was still staring across the bay at Alcatraz Island and I waited for him to say something else.

"Diana passed away on June twentieth, 2006. Today is June twentieth 2007. After she died I knew exactly what needed to be done. We had talked about this many times throughout our marriage. Diana was to be cremated and her ashes were to be taken to Alcatraz. She loved that island and her happiest moments were spent on that island. I couldn't let go of her, and although I did have her cremated as I promised her I would, I couldn't bring myself to take her to Alcatraz. It's been a year and I realize now that I must fulfill her wishes.

"Tina, I needed you to be here because you know details about me that no one else knows. I invited you into my life and that included the most intimate parts of my life. My children, my close friends and my family will be here tomorrow, but even they don't fully understand what Diana meant to me. You will be the only person there that never even met Diana, yet you knew the part of her that she only shared with me. I needed you to be here because you're the only one that understands. If I were to leave this world I would be leaving knowing that someone out there knows my story. And no matter what, my story is not finished until I have said goodbye to the love of my life. Diana saved my life and she never even knew it."

I was trying to absorb all that C.J. was saying and although a lot of my questions were being answered I found myself with new concerns. *Was C.J. contemplating suicide? Was he now leaving Diana at Alcatraz because he knew he would be joining her? What do I do? What do I say?*

Before I had a chance to say anything C.J. turned away from Alcatraz placed his hand in mine and we began walking. Our walk back to the hotel was silent and as we approached the front of the hotel C.J. squeezed my hand, gently kissed me on the cheek and said goodnight.

I took the elevator back up to my room and once inside I made my way to the safe. I frantically grabbed for the file folder. Maybe I had missed something.

Chapter 6
Searching for Clues

03/14/07

My dear friend,

As I write to you this evening I am exhausted, and although my body is telling me to sleep, my mind won't allow it.

I spent yet another day rummaging through old letters, photographs and memento's. Organizing this office of mine is taking much longer than I had originally anticipated, but I find myself enjoying the process. So many wonderful things to re-discover; pieces of a life that would have no meaning or worth to anyone besides myself.

I found a packet of photo's dated August 1977 and as I pulled them out I realized that they were from a trip to Hawaii that Diana and I took to celebrate our tenth wedding anniversary.

One photo in particular caught my eye and after staring at it for nearly an hour I closed my eye's and remembered the evening it was taken.

Diana and I had spent this particular day in Oahu moving at our own pace. As we drove along the north shore Diana perked up and suggested we visit the rainforest. At first l was rather critical of her choice, but the smile on her face turned my criticism into willingness.

We made our way to the rainforest, parked the car and began walking. The tree's were the most vibrant shade of green that I had ever seen and before long we found ourselves in a down pour.

We had spotted a group, all wearing rain poncho's, and I commented to Diana that we should have taken a guided tour. Diana smiled her usual coy smile and we continued our walk.

There were places on the trail that we were following that were extremely rocky and to say they were slippery would truly be an understatement, but we laughed and continued the path that we were on.

Suddenly, there in the quiet of the forest, we heard rushing water. With each step that we took the sound of rushing water became louder. And then, there it was...a magnificent waterfall! Diana was beaming and within moments we found ourselves alone. The last of the tour group was making their way back to their tour bus and Diana pulled me close to her.

I wrapped my arms around Diana and I felt her body begin to tremble. We kissed, softly at first, and then my tongue met hers. I felt Diana's hands run up my back and as they made their way back down she applied more pressure. As we continued to kiss I moved my hands from her waist up to her breasts and felt her hard nipples through her tank top. I broke from our kiss and slowly ran my tongue down her neck. Diana's hands were now on my waist and she undid the snap on my jeans. I slowly pulled her shirt over her head, lowered my head to her breasts and pulled her nipple into my mouth. I ran my tongue between her breasts and then pulled the other nipple into my mouth.

Diana was moaning and as I alternated between her breasts I let my hands slowly run down her body and unsnapped and unzipped her shorts. I ran my tongue down her stomach and with my hands on her ass I pulled her closer to my mouth.

The rain continued to pour and the sound of the waterfall was intoxicating. Diana ran her hands through my hair and as she reached orgasm her hold became tighter.

I ran my tongue back up across her stomach and then paused for a moment to once again pull each of her nipples into my mouth. My tongue then ran across her neck and our lips met.

Diana began to unbutton my shirt and her hands ran down my chest. I kept my eye's closed as Diana softly kissed my chest and her hands pulled at my jeans. Even through the rain and the thunder from the waterfall I could hear Diana breathing. I felt a tightness in my stomach and as Diana took me into her mouth I felt dizzy.

My hands were placed on the back of her head and as I ran them through her wet hair I was overcome with the love I felt for this woman. I was thankful for the rain because Diana never knew that tears had been running down my face.

Diana's ability to bring me to new levels of ecstasy has never failed to amaze me.

The photo that I'm including was shot immediately after we returned to our car. I look at it today and it brings back every moment we spent in the rainforest.

I now am ready for sleep.

Much love,

C.J.

03/29/07

Hello!

I am thrilled to report that I have finally completed the task of organizing my home office. Although the bulk of the work is now complete I find myself with stacks of pictures, letters and greeting cards that I have absolutely no idea what to do with.

I thought about placing these life long mementos' in a trunk, a time capsule if you will, for our children to discover some day. But, for now they are in tidy stacks and I find myself spending hours each and every day reminiscing.

I have come to understand and appreciate the amazing gift God has given us; the gift of memory. It's simply incredible that we have the ability to close our eyes and travel back in time. I had never really thought about it before, but I have a new appreciation for this sense. My heart goes out to those suffering from Alzheimer's disease. I cannot imagine waking up tomorrow and not being able to remember. I am thankful for so many things in life, but my memory... nothing makes me more thankful than that.

Love C.J.

04/10/07

Hello!

I hope you are doing well, and I wanted to tell you that I enjoyed the photo's of your trip to Mexico! The various shots of the sunsets were breath taking.

My last trip to Mexico was in 1990. Our daughter, Isabella, had left home for college and Diana and I found ourselves home alone. With each and every passing day the house seemed to grow more quiet than it had been the day before.

Diana and I enjoyed our new found freedom and the luxuries that came with that freedom, but we both felt the need to just get away. It was there, in Mexico, that for the first time in my life I thought my marriage was over.

Diana and I were lying in bed after making love for hours when I felt my chest becoming wet. I realized that Diana was crying. I asked her what was wrong and as she ran her hand across my stomach she asked me if I had ever cheated on her. My mind began to race and I was trying to figure out if she knew something. I suddenly was terrified. Had she known all along? Had she kept quiet until the kids were out of the house? In my uncontrollable panic I became angry. I told her in no uncertain terms that I had never cheated on her and I couldn't believe she would even ask me such a thing. Why? Had she cheated on me?

Immediately after asking her that question I wished I hadn't. In my attempt to cover up my own infidelity I was forced to face hers.

Yes, Diana had been unfaithful. I was angry, I was hurt, and I was terrified. I hated her for telling me. I had loved her enough to not hurt her this way, but in an attempt to clear her own conscience she destroyed me.

Diana apologized over and over and her tears were like a water faucet that couldn't be turned off. She regretted her actions and she begged me to listen to her and to try to understand. Then came the words that I never thought I would hear come from my wife's mouth: It was only sex.

Only sex? No it wasn't. Now she's lying to me. I know Diana…I know women. Women cheat because something is missing in their lives. Men cheat because they crave the excitement; the chase. Women make love with their minds. My wife made love to another man! I took one good look at Diana, got dressed and left her there to console herself. If she was looking for forgiveness she wasn't going to get it from me.

I left the hotel and walked for what seemed like miles. I kept playing a video in my head and I didn't like what I was seeing. Diana and some faceless son of a bitch making love. Laughing. Holding each other. I saw her body being pleasured by a man that wasn't me.

The further I walked the angrier I became. I wanted to go back and tell Diana that she had no right to tell me this. She had no right to cleanse herself of guilt at my expense. Why couldn't she respect me the way I had respected her? Just because two people are married to each other doesn't mean they have to know the details of each others lives. Especially when those details are capable of destroying a life time of love. Capable of destroying a family. Just who the hell did she think she was?

I never did go back to the hotel that night. I found a bar and did what any man would have done; I got drunk. I woke up the next morning on the beach and made my way back to our room.

Diana was sitting in a chair and her eyes were puffy. She started to apologize again and begged me to talk to her. For the first time in my life I looked at Diana and saw someone that I couldn't stand to look at.

I took a shower, got dressed and instructed Diana to start packing her things. We were going home, or at least she was. I didn't know if I could ever go home again. One thing was for certain, we weren't going to stay in Mexico.

Not a word was spoken between Diana and myself on our trip back to San Francisco. Once home I packed my things, loaded them into my car and left Diana there alone.

For two weeks I stayed in a hotel. I never called Diana and refused to return her calls. There was nothing that she could say that could possibly make this right.

Then one evening, after having way too much to drink, I found myself lying in this hotel bed, eyes closed, trying to fathom how this happened. I kept thinking about it. Envisioning it. Replaying that damn video in my head over and over again.

It was sometime after midnight that it suddenly became clear to me. I loved her. I missed her. I was overcome with sorrow and and I couldn't stop the tears.

Diana had made a mistake and in Diana's own way she told me because she loved me. She never could keep a secret and she loved me enough to sacrifice everything. I jumped up, grabbed my car keys and went home.

When I arrived Diana was sound asleep. I sat down in the chair next to her side of the bed and watched her sleep. I was still sitting there when she woke up that morning.

I told Diana that I didn't want to know who, but if there was a problem within our marriage I needed her to tell me how to make it right. I needed to know what she wasn't getting from me that would lead her to another mans bed.

We cried and talked for hours and I learned something about my wife that day. I learned that loving a woman more than life itself isn't enough. I learned that even the most beautiful women in the world can feel insecure. I learned that women want and need to feel like they've been heard.

I always complimented my wife. My attraction for her never waned. But I never knew that as she was growing older she was growing insecure and unsure of herself. She needed to feel alive and as much as I had loved her, she only felt like a wife.

I never looked at Diana the same way again. I had been looking at her for years as my wife, but from that day forward I looked at her as a woman. A woman who needed excitement in her life. A woman who needed to talk to me about more than the bills, the children, or household chores.

Our marriage had always been good and our sex life had always been amazing, but somehow life happened, and I was guilty. Guilty of taking this woman for granted. Guilty of assuming that she belonged to me. Guilty of forgetting that she wasn't just a wife and mother, but a beautiful woman that didn't need me, but wanted me.

Yes my dear, I was guilty! And I was more than happy to serve a life sentence.

Diana and I never discussed her infidelity again. Truth be known, I did on occasion think about it, but no longer did

I think about it as a terrible event in our lives. I changed my way of thinking and now when I recall that trip to Mexico I see it as a defining moment in our marriage. Without Diana's brief encounter with another man I may have never known the woman that she was becoming. I could have lived the rest of my life with my "wife." But instead, I have lived my life with an incredible woman.

Adios ~ C.J.

04/17/07

Dear Tina,

Just a quick note to say hello and let you know that I will be MIA for the next couple of weeks. I'm not sure if you remember me talking about my old friend Mark, but he was one of the guys that I use to go on annual hunting and fishing trips with.

Unfortunately, his wife passed away recently and he has had a difficult time of it.

Mark now lives in Canada and after a long telephone conversation he has convinced me to come up and do a bit of fishing. Well, we're not really fisherman; that's just man code for "Hey, lets get together and drink ourselves into oblivion!" It's been a few years since we've seen each other, and I think the trip may do us both some good.

Take care and I will be in touch!

Much love

C.J.

05/02/07

Hello My Dear!

I must say, as much as I enjoyed my trip to Canada, I missed logging on to my computer and finding a new e-mail from you.

As predicted, Mark and I never even got close to a fishing pole, but we surely had a wonderful time! If we weren't sitting in our cabin drinking and telling "war stories" then we were bar hopping and perfecting our "people skills."

I found myself missing Diana more often than I care to mention, and I must confess, without her there I found my old ways creeping back in.

We had been at the lake for a week and I was enjoying my daily morning walk. I had a bit of a hangover, but the weather was cool and crisp and I was beginning to feel much better. As I made my way around the lake I noticed a woman walking toward me and as my eyes met hers I greeted her with a simple "Good morning!" She smiled and returned the greeting. When I returned from my walk I saw the same woman sitting on the steps of the cabin next door to mine. She smiled and said "Well hello again!" I walked towards her and she raised her coffee cup and asked me if I would like to join her. I accepted her offer and we spent the next hour sitting there on that porch chatting away.

I found myself drawn to this woman and her eyes made me smile. As it turned out, she was there on vacation with her sister, and she was recently divorced.

I never told her that I was married, but I didn't try to hide it either. After all, my wedding ring never leaves my finger. I don't think it mattered to her one way or the other. She was smiling and flirting and I have no doubt that a blind man could have seen what she had on her mind.

I thanked her for the coffee and the conversation and as I stood up to leave she invited me to join her for dinner that evening. Part of my brain (the part that knows better) was telling me to decline this offer, but the other part of my brain (the part that has caused me to do stupid things my entire life) told me to accept. I guess you already know which part I listened to.

Later that evening I walked over to her cabin and knocked on the door. Her sister answered, invited me in, and then called out to Jessica "All right then. I'm leaving! Have a good night!" She said goodbye to me and walked out the door.

Jessica called out to me telling me she was running a few minutes late, but she would be right out. I should make myself at home and help myself to a drink.

The cabin was laid out exactly as mine, so I went into the kitchen and grabbed a beer from the fridge. As I turned from the fridge to make my way back into the living room I noticed Jessica standing there.

There are some things in life that never change and the appreciation for a beautiful woman is one of them.

Jessica's light brown hair fell slightly above her shoulders and her brown eyes seemed to sparkle. I didn't know her age, but if I were to guess I would put her at 35. She was thin, but not bone thin, and although I hadn't noticed earlier that morning I now noticed her legs. Jessica was wearing a green button down blouse, that was unbuttoned to show her cleavage. It was loosely tucked inside her jeans that showed exactly how long her legs were. Add in the fact that she was wearing 2 - 3 inch heels and I knew those legs led straight to heaven.

I offered to grab a beer for her, but she declined. There was a chilled bottle of wine in the fridge and she preferred that. I opened the fridge to get the bottle of wine and Jessica moved past me to get a wine glass. I poured the wine for her and we walked into the living room.

We made a bit of small talk and then Jessica suggested that perhaps we stay in for the evening. She was sure we could find something in the kitchen to eat. I was fairly confident on how this evening was going to play out so I agreed. Jessica kicked off her shoes and we continued our small talk; me with another beer and Jessica with another glass of wine.

Our conversation was flowing as if we had known each other for a long time. As Jessica spoke her eyes gazed into mine and at times I felt the urge to lean over and kiss her, but I didn't. I pushed that urge back deciding that if anything between Jessica and myself was going to happen it would happen because that's what she wanted.

We continued to drink and talk and then Jessica ran her hand through her hair and leaned in close to me. As she lifted her eyes to look into mine I felt that familiar stir.

I pulled Jessica to me and our lips met. I ran my fingers up and down her arm and she moved her hand across my thigh. I continued to kiss her and then slowly moved to her neck. Jessica moaned and she placed my hand on her breast. Her nipple was hard and as I eased her on her back I continued to kiss her neck and work my way down. I slowly unbuttoned her blouse and allowed my lips and tongue to wander across her body. I then moved my hand to her waist and began to unbutton her jeans. Once her

129

jeans were unbuttoned and unzipped Jessica raised her hips and I pulled them off her body.

Jessica's breathing had become quicker and she pulled my shirt over my head. I lowered myself on top of Jessica and felt the warmth of her body. Our kisses were no longer soft; they had become more passionate and as my tongue circled around hers I could feel her hand unbutton and then unzip my jeans. She moved to her side and then gently pushed me so that I was lying on my back. Jessica pulled my jeans off and ran her tongue up my thigh and all the way back up to my neck.

Jessica was on top of me and I watched her face as we finally came together. She threw her head back and my eyes traveled from her face down to her breasts, and then across her flat stomach.

As our movement became quicker I closed my eyes and listened to Jessica's whimpers. I was deep inside her and struggled to catch my breath. Jessica reached orgasm and I followed shortly afterward.

My body felt exhausted, but I wanted and needed to continue. Jessica took me by the hand and led me into her bedroom. I laid her down on the bed and felt her body quiver as I once again entered her. We moved together in perfect rhythm and Jessica's hands moved up my arms and down my chest. I lowered my head and our lips once again met.

We made love for several hours that night and after she had fallen asleep I quietly left the room, got dressed and let myself out.

Once back at my cabin I undressed and showered. As the hot water hit my skin I cried. I was overcome with emotion and for the first time in my adult life I felt guilty for experiencing such pleasure with anyone other than Diana.

You may not understand this now, but in time you will. It has been my nature, my desire, my addiction that has led me to find pleasure outside my marriage, but I had always reasoned that it was just sex. This was the first time that I understood completely that it is not just sex. It's a meeting of two minds, two bodies and two souls. My mind, body and soul belong to Diana.

05/15/07

Dear Tina,

I'm writing to you today from my daughters home in San Diego. I received a phone call from her day before yesterday informing me that she had kicked her husband out of the house. She was crying and I could hear my grandchildren in the background. I didn't know why she had kicked him out of the house, and she made no attempt to tell me, but I had the feeling that I should come down and try to help her through this difficult time.

Last night Isabella told me that she had caught Michael cheating on her. It wasn't just a suspicion, or a telephone number in his wallet, but she had actually caught him. She came home early from work and found Michael in her bed with another woman.

As a father I wanted to track him down and beat the living hell out of him, but as a man all I could think was "what a dumb ass... he can't even cheat right!"

Of course I told Isabella that she deserved better than that and if he couldn't be faithful then he wasn't worthy of her love. But inside, I wanted to tell her something all together different. I wanted to tell her that his cheating had nothing to do with her. I wanted to tell her that she should give him a break and realize that he was just doing what men do; acting on male instinct. We are born with an uncontrollable instinct that tells us to merge with the opposite sex.

I have often wondered if monogamy is at all natural. How could anyone be expected to find a single mate and stay with that one person for the remainder of their lives?

I realize that I go back and forth on this, but I think my stand on the issue varies depending on what I'm feeling on any given day.

It's the same old problem that I have dealt with my entire life. Loving one person, but still having the need and desire to experience pleasure with another.

I wanted to tell Isabella that the fact that he took pleasure with another woman has absolutely nothing to do with his love for her. I wanted to make her understand how a man thinks.

This was my opportunity to share with Isabella a part of myself. To help her. To give her information that most people, or more importantly, most women, don't get. I could have sat her down and explained how I have learned why I do the things I do. I could have told her about my own struggles. I could have explained to her the love that I have for her mother and the amazing marriage that we have had, yet I never stopped indulging my own sexual urges. Maybe that would have helped Isabella understand her own husband. But, I did not.

I feel that I have done my daughter a great disservice. I could have spoken to her as a man to a woman, but I did not. Instead, I spoke to her as a father to a daughter. I attempted to build her up by knocking Michael down. I told her that he was immature and didn't understand how his actions affected the lives of others. I told her that she deserved better than a cheating husband that would allow another woman into their bed. I even went as far as to use a Dr. Phil line...I actually told her that you don't solve marital problems by going outside the marriage. As I said those words I wanted to kick my own ass! A man doesn't necessarily cheat because there are marital problems! Dr. Phil should know that!

133

So, in closing, I screwed up. I'm going to stay here a few more days and spend time with the kids. If I grow a set large enough to tell Isabella the truth about men I will let you know.

C.J.

06/01/07

Dear friend,

I am writing to you today to request a favor. I will understand if you can't find a way, but if you can I will forever be grateful.

As you know, Diana and I have not been to Alcatraz Island since moving Jake and Sandra out back in 1971. I vowed to never go back there, and to date I have remained true to that vow.

However, Diana wants to go back. She wants all of us there one last time. The children will be coming home, along with our grandchildren. A few close friends as well as other family members will be there. Tina, I feel as close to you, if not closer, than those that I have known a lifetime.

So, I am requesting your appearance. We will be visiting Alcatraz Island on June 20, 2007 at 10:00 am.

Should you find a way to join us please give me a call. I will be more than happy to make any and all arrangements for you.

Love C.J.

Chapter 7
The "Aha" Moment

I looked over at the clock sitting on the bedside table and realized that I had spent the entire night reading C.J.'s letters. It was now 8am and time was running out. In two hours I will be joining C.J., his family and his closest friends as Diana is laid to rest.

I still don't know what to do. I'm shocked that I never caught on to what C.J. had been telling me. He even wrote to me the day Diana had died. Reading that letter again brought tears to my eyes. C. J. spoke of making love to Diana the day before she died. He had been so upset that he didn't tell her he loved her that morning, yet they spent the entire previous day making love.

How did I miss the fact that he didn't mention Diana being there when he visited Isabella? A mother would have been there to support her daughter during a time such as that.

The two month absence...C.J. had not written for two months, and when he finally did, the tone of his letters had changed.

The night he spent with Jessica. He was emotionally devastated afterwards. How did I not see that he hadn't been cheating on Diana, but rather her memory?

I tried to put all the pieces together, but what I couldn't shake was the feeling of doom. C.J. had been getting his affairs in order. Taking the time to organize his home office. He had, on more than one occasion, mentioned *his story*. What he wanted his children to know, and the importance of "coming clean" seemed to be eating at him.

Had C.J. set me up to tell his story? The story that he didn't have the courage to tell, but wanted his children to know? Was this all part of a plan? And, if it was, then how do I stop it?

137

I couldn't stop worrying and my hands were shaking. I had spent the entire night smoking one cigarette after the other and my head was pounding. I knew that I had to talk to C.J. and if it meant postponing my trip back home then so be it.

I showered, dressed and attempted to put on my make up. My hands were shaking uncontrollably and after two failed attempts I decided to forego the make up. A little moisturizer, a little bronzer and I was good to go.

I was as ready as I was going to be. I placed CJ's letters back into the file folder and then placed the file folder into the safe. I grabbed my purse and walked out the door.

As I approached pier 39 I spotted C.J. He was smiling and I couldn't help but to notice how youthful he looked. His eye's had a sparkle and he radiated a warm glow.

Several people were standing around him and several more were gathered in small groups. I noticed C.J. was wearing black dress pants and a white dress shirt. I also noticed a red ribbon pin placed right above his heart.

I walked over to where C.J. was standing and he placed his arm around me. I was introduced to those that he had been speaking with and after the introductions he excused himself.

Moments later C.J. was back and he was holding hands with a woman who looked eerily familiar to me. It was Isabella. I was taken back by the similarity between her and Diana. She was the spitting image of Diana the day she married C.J.

"Tina! This is my daughter, Isabella. Isabella, this is Tina, a very dear friend of mine!" C.J. seemed pleased that we were here at the same time, the same place, and for the same reason. Isabella extended her hand and thanked me for coming.

As more people arrived I lost track of CJ. For a brief moment I felt as if I were at a family reunion, but it wasn't my family. People were hugging each other and talking as old friends do. Catching up on the latest gossip, complaining of old ailments and new one's. I smiled politely and answered questions as they arose.

Isabella was standing a few feet away from me and I watched as her little girl walked over and placed her hand in Isabella's. I imagined that Diana had probably stood in this exact location many years ago holding Isabella's hand.

I suddenly felt a hand on my shoulder and turned to find C.J. standing there.

"Tina, come with me! My son just arrived and I want to introduce the two of you!"

C.J. and I began to walk toward a group of people standing near the edge of the pier. A man approximately CJ's height and weight had his back to us. C.J. placed his hand on his son's shoulder and I heard him say "If I can steal you for a moment, there's someone I want you to meet."

The gentleman turned around to face me and my smile quickly turned to disbelief. Judging by the look on his face he was as confused as I was. His mouth opened and before C.J. could say anything he spoke up. "Tina? What are you doing here?"

My hands began to shake and I felt a lump in my throat. Only one word came to mind, one name. I couldn't breathe and my head felt like it was going to explode.

"Chuck?"

Printed in Great Britain
by Amazon.co.uk, Ltd.,
Marston Gate.